IT SHOULD'VE BEEN ME

EVALEE SERIES

BECCA SIMONE

CONTENTS

1

Privilege is granted at birth, but I will never taste the privilege that was stolen from me the moment my parents conceived me. In the grand scheme of things, some might say I am more privileged than most of the world, and while that is true, it doesn't change my circumstances in modern-day America.

So, I gave up on privilege long ago and decided to be a fighter. I was going to fight for everything I wanted, everything I needed, and everything I deserved, and in many ways, I preferred it that way.

But the one thing I asked for, if I wasn't granted privilege, was fairness. So, fairness became my standard. If I fought and worked hard at something, I'd expected to see my hard work pay off and for most of my life, it did. Until today.

Today privilege won, and it won in the form of lineage.

The news broke today in an eleven o'clock email from the CEO of Business Solutions Group(BSG), Deirdra Scottfield.

My Caesar salad delicately crafted by some convenient store employee sat on the table untouched. The desire to eat passed the moment I read the email.

My eyes gravitated to my best friend, Sara, who was currently reading the email. Her green eyes moved from left to right, like the paper in a typewriter. She concluded her reading with a heavy sigh and bit her bottom lip.

She slid my laptop back. "I am sorry, Olivia. I know you worked really hard for that director position."

"Yes, but commitment doesn't matter to this company. I just wish I knew that six years ago when I applied." I closed my laptop and slid it into my bag. "I did everything right, didn't I? I showed expertise and became well-rounded in other departments. I worked overtime and weekends. I expanded the company's client portfolio by fifteen percent. I am both a team player and the department manager. I—"

My voice wobbled so much that I couldn't finish the sentence.

Sara noticed. "Olivia, are you okay?"

"Can you— can you distract me?" I muttered.

"Huh?"

"Distract me. I need to think about something else before I break down in tears. Talk about anything; the moon, your sister, dating. That's it, talk about dating!"

Sara's eyes widened. She knew I had to be desperate if I asked her to talk about dating. Any other day, I prefer not to spend our lunch discussing why I didn't want to go on a coffee date with Brad from tech, or Zayn from Sales, and definitely not Sam from HR. I don't even think Sam from HR was allowed. But today I allowed it.

Sara tilted her head toward me, determining if I was joking or not.

"Seriously, let's talk about dating. Match me. Go crazy."

"Well, only because you asked." She smiled. "There has to be someone in our 150-person company that suits you." She took another bite of her kale salad and thought. "How about this—

we'll go to the next happy hour. It'll probably be at that new Mediterranean spot that just opened down the street." She gasps. "Oh, I know! Let me do your makeup."

"Hard pass."

"Oh come on, you have so much untapped potential!" she squealed. "I would die for your bouncy banana curls and your warm caramel skin."

She couldn't understand why, though I explained many times to her. Men didn't want my type. Men had a one-track mind. They had an idea of what beauty was, and it wasn't black banana curls. It was pin-straight hair, preferably blonde, though brown was passable. In this case, I had neither. And don't get me started on the skin, The second I walk into the room, I am labeled and tossed into the *I would never* date category.

Sure, I've dated here and there, but that's exactly how far it would go—a date and then ghosted. I was never "good enough" to continue to date, let alone get into a relationship, and God forbid married to. So, I gave up on that long ago. I just wish Sara would.

In her defense, her matchmaker nature wasn't her fault. She was always the hopeless romantic one and after coming back from her honeymoon last month she was determined to find me a suitable match.

I clipped up my curly hair—the hair that Sara admired so much—and leaned back in the chair. The whole relationship thing never bothered me either; I was never one to concern myself with my dating status. I had a comfortable life in my one-bedroom apartment on the edge of the city, with my six-year-old tabby cat, Link, and the goldfish that I won from a carnival. There was no way I needed some man to come and disturb my life.

I sipped my seltzer and watched Sara intently scroll through our company's website looking for suitable contenders.

Maybe I do regret this.

"Hey, how was your Vermont trip last weekend? I forgot to ask."

Sara head popped up like the Whack-a-Mole game. The tense skin between her eyebrows relaxed.

"Aww, Olivia it was beautiful. James surprised me with a beautiful cottage, rose bouquet, and massage. We went hiking, apple picking, and—"

She stopped midway and melted into her memories. Sara was completely and utterly in love. She blushed at some parts of the stories and giggled at others. I had a feeling she'd be in her newlywed phase for a long time.

"Okay, girl, we need to head back." I picked up my phone to show her. "It's about to be one o'clock."

She whined as she threw her things in a bag and pushed in her chair. "We'll be on time. The building is right there." She pointed up.

"If I am on time, it means I am late, that's what my dad would say." I looped my arm through hers and we walked in the direction of the building.

It was a subtle gesture, but one with intention. Sara always found a way to get distracted. Whether it's shopping, chatting, and more recently, trying to find me a date.

We strolled back inside to the lobby. Dale, the doorman, looked up from his watch.

"Ms. Olivia, you never come back this late from lunch." He smiled. "As the company's most timely employee, I do have to say how disappointed I am."

I frowned at Sara, who heard the comment as well.

"Oh, you take things too seriously, Olivia." Sara giggled. "You know Dale likes to tease."

The two of them continued to chat about my unattractive obsessions while I grabbed my key card, and scanned in.

"C'mon, Sara." I waved. "I have projects, and deadlines, and meetings."

"Projects, deadlines, and meetings, oh my," she teased and scanned in.

I rolled my eyes. "You know, I talked to your lead this morning; looks like your team is swamped with work as well."

"And look, am I stressed? Nope." She used the back of her phone case as a mirror to reapply her candy apple red lipstick. "Want some?" She held the phone over to me.

I took it from her, knowing exactly what I was about to see. A bare and unexciting face, just the way I liked it. I didn't have time for makeup in the morning and didn't need the attention from it either.

"Nope." I passed the phone back to her. "I look great."

"You do look great," she whispered. "You're naturally beautiful. So, why don't you use that beauty to get yourself on a hot date, huh?"

The elevator dinged and opened its door to the sixth floor.

"Okay Sara. See you later." I gently pushed her out and smiled at the perfect timing.

Her face twisted to an evil glare. Whatever she was plotting was too late as the elevator door was starting to close.

"She's single!" Sara yelled as she pointed directly to me in an elevator filled with men.

Oh, I hate her.

The door shut and heat rushed to my face, my armpits were suddenly moist, and I became acutely aware of myself.

I moved to the back of the elevator and hid from the staring and confused faces. Growing up, I hated attention, and now that I'm grown I still hate it. In fact it's gotten worse.

The elevator dinged and I quickly excused myself from the uncomfortable situation. Several heads shot up from their cubicle to see who it was. Once they saw it was only me, they sank back down in disappointment.

Weird.

I sat down and began my office routine: turn on the feet heater, refill my water bottle. Stretch. Listen to voicemails. Check emails.

I opened the first email:

HELLO BSG FAMILY,

We ask you to help us extend a warm welcome to our new Director of Operations, Luca Lontern. Luca has over a decade of experience in department collaborations, extensive knowledge of the business solutions industry, and achieving the company's short- and long-term objectives.

He has requested a four p.m. meet-and-greet with all employees in the lower-level faculty room. All employees are required to attend the meeting and will end their day after.

On behalf of the board and myself we look forward to welcoming Luca in his new chapter at BSG.

Best Regards,

Deirdra B. Scottfield

CEO of Business Solutions Group

MY STOMACH DROPPED as my earlier feelings resurfaced. Sara did a good job distracting me from the whole director situation. I had completely forgotten about it until now. Maybe I didn't regret talking about dating as much as I said I did.

"How did they not pick you?" I heard a voice say behind me. The voice belongs to one of my team leads, Oscar. He was leaning over my cubicle while still sipping his Starbucks Frappuccino.

I ignored Oscar's question completely as I wasn't emotionally ready to answer it.

Oscar started working here three years ago. He was a fairly thin middle-aged man who had been catfished too many times to count. His work was minimal, but he always got it done. Despite knowing his workload could be heavier and faster, for some reason I liked him. Maybe because he was easygoing, or because he stayed late with me to achieve the department goals when no one else would. Regardless, Oscar along with Sara were the ones that knew I was going for the Director position. They were my core family here.

"Is that why everyone stared at me when I came in? They thought I was *him*—the new director."

He nodded. "They've been talking about it since the email dropped. Maybe we'll see this Luca guy more than Chris."

Our last director, Chris Scottfield, had left due to him "wanting to spend more time with his family", as the company email had stated. However, people in the office would say, "Bologna!"

There were many theories surrounding Chris's unexpected departure. Sara, like many others, said he was secretly fired, but I knew he wasn't. His great grandfather founded the company and therefore established his bloodline to run through the company's veins. The more reasonable theory was that the board asked him to step down, due to his lack of knowledge of the business and consistent absences.

Family companies who hired their offspring were my biggest pet peeves. While hiring your son or daughter is not evidently bad, most of them have no actual desire for the business, at least not to the extent of their grandparents. So, they will work in the company, but out of some unspoken duty to honor the family's name.

Oscar sighed. "Luca requested a four p.m. meet-and-greet with all employees. I dislike him already."

"I would rather work on my other projects. How is he the Director of Operations and he's requesting that we all adjust our schedule to suck up to him? What an effective way to waste time."

Oscar raised his eyebrow and laughed at my frustration. "I know you had things planned for that hour. Did Luca ruin them?"

"Yes," I whined. "We were going to go over that campaign for Cosmetic X this afternoon. Then I was going to look over some presentations, and I will definitely miss sending out my afternoon emails. Luca is the death of me already. "

"Let's plan for Friday morning," Oscar offered.

"Let me check." I opened my Friday calendar. I could feel his body heat hovering over me. He couldn't help but peek over at my schedule.

"Eww, you follow that?"

I nudged him away. "Yes, it keeps me organized and on task."

"But why are there so many colors?"

I spun my chair around to face him. This was a question I didn't mind answering. "Red means it hasn't started. Yellow means 'pending'. Green means 'done.' and blue means 'needs attention.' It's my color code system. I can make one for you, if you'd like."

He shook his head in disgust. "Hard pass. So, can you fit the Cosmetics X campaign in tomorrow morning or not?"

"So, tomorrow morning's schedule is already set and color coded. I'd have to move several tasks around to accommodate Sir Luca, his Majesty, but it is possible."

"Great." Oscar clapped his hands. "Let's wrap up early today so we can head to the meet-and-greet."

I rolled my eyes and began rearranging my schedule. "Right, this is so great."

• • •

"Ahh, you two made it!" Sara waved us down. She was at the entryway of the faculty room.

"Sara, we're not at some concert, we have to be here," I scolded.

She looped her arm through mine as if we were high school BFF's walking into class together. "I know, Olivia, but the company set up refreshments inside, and we can go home after this meeting concludes. This is just as good as a concert. And why are you wearing that?" She referred to my outfit.

"Uh, you mean what I came to work in? Then yes, I am wearing my striped button-down top with my gray pencil skirt and beige flats. I am not going home to change for some meet-and-greet for our new director."

"Listen, all I'm saying is that you need a little oomph some-times, especially if you're meeting the new boss. Use your emer-gency outfit that you store in your car. Don't you agree, Oscar?"

I shot Oscar a look. I hated when these two were together. They were too similar in so many ways, and it drove me insane.

Oscar grinned, knowing exactly what he was going to do. "You know Sara. I told her the same exact thing. How will she ever attract a man and get married if she looks like a middle school principal? She definitely needs your consulting."

I hate you, I mouthed to him.

"Thank you, Oscar." Sara smiled. "This is what I've been telling her all along, but she looks at me like I have five heads."

She stepped back and held her chin as she thought of ways to sexualize me.

"Why don't we just loosen up your hair? Unbutton a couple of buttons on top? And maybe—"

"Absolutely not! Why would I want a man that looks at me for that!?" I said a little too loudly.

Several men turned in my direction. "Come on, let's just get this meeting over with." I headed inside to what sounded like a high school cafeteria.

Oscar headed straight for the refreshments table and told us to save him a seat. I scanned the room for an open table with three empty seats closest to the exit door and certainly out of sight of the speaker.

When I found one, I beelined straight for it, weaving through the crowds of tech nerds and the arrogant sales employees. From the corner of my eye, I could see Brenda from the billing department and her team trailing behind her, aiming for the same spot I was.

I reached the table and immediately plopped down on the chair, marking my victory.

Brenda huffed and rolled her eyes. "It isn't a race, Olivia."

"Then why were you also running?"

She spun around to her team. "Let's find another table. Consultants here are just extra employees here that take up space."

She left and Sara and Oscar finally caught up. "We're so far away from the front," she frowned.

"Exactly," I nodded, and checked my watch. "If this goes by quickly, I might still have time to finish up that Cosmetics X campaign."

"Nope!" Oscar cut in. "We already discussed that we will leave that for tomorrow morning."

Oscar and Sara went back to chatting, while the room slowly began to settle as people found their seats.

I spotted Deirdra in front. It was never hard to find her—

thin, tall, and blonde. Not to mention she was always in white no matter the event, no matter the location, and no matter the season. White was her signature color. She reminded me of my mother, who was stuck in the seventies with too much hair product and one hundred bobby pins in her hair.

But, even in her mid-fifties she found a way to grab the male gaze with just a strut across the stage.

"Welcome BSG family, I'd like to thank everyone for coming. I know since the departure of Chris, everyone has been eagerly awaiting his replacement."

Oscar bent over to me. "No, we haven't," he whispered.

I playfully flicked his knee, hinting at him to be quiet. Sara caught wind and chuckled.

"Shh," we heard from our left. The "shh" was so loud it caught Deirdra off guard, and she had to briefly pause. I peeked over to see that it came from Brenda. She squinted her eyes at us and swung her body around to face the front, like a teacher's pet trying to earn brownie points.

With the sea of people, Deirdra didn't know who interrupted her, so she continued. "Without further ado, it is my pleasure to introduce to you the new Director of Operations, my nephew Luca Lontern."

This is part two where life isn't fair. Out of everything I've done for the company—the long nights, the countless meetings, the free weekend work—this is the part where no matter what you do, the reward goes to someone who didn't put in as much work as I did to get the job, and of course it's her nephew.

A round of applause was requested upon Luca's walk to the podium, and while the room echoed with hundreds of claps, including from Sara and Oscar, I couldn't bring myself to do it.

From the corner of the room, a tall man appeared. He was dressed to the nines in a suit and tie and loafers, as expected. He kept one hand in his pocket, while giving a single wave to the crowd. Once he got to the podium he turned to face us, and I knew.

Sara gave me sloppy hits to the thigh. "Oh my—Olivia."

I leaned closer to her. "Don't you start, especially not with him."

"But he has that coveted dark hair, he's tall, and do I spot a defined jawline on him?" She grabbed my arms in excitement. "If only we were sitting closer we would catch his eye color. I bet it's blue like Deirdra's."

"Ouch, you're digging your nails into my arms," I said, peeling her fingers off me, but she was too mesmerized by her delusion of a future between Luca and me.

"Good afternoon, all." His amplified deep voice startled me. I wasn't expecting it to be as deep as it was.

"I will keep this short, as I am sure that many of you saw this as an opportunity as a quick chance to show up, as long as it meant getting to go home early. I am honored to have such an opportunity to work for not only my family, but for what my great grandfather built. I promise throughout the duration of my employment to achieve and deliver all that this position requires of me. There is not enough time in this short meet-and-greet to get to know all of you, so I hope in the days, months, and even years ahead that I will get to know each one of you as we work toward the same goal my great grandfather built so many years ago. Thank you."

A second round of applause followed his ending statement, and shortly afterward people were swarming around him.

"Hey, look, he's definitely related." Sara tilted her phone in my direction. She's been snooping on their social media the entire time. "Scottfield is his mom's maiden name, but he obviously took the last name of his dad which was Lontern."

She tried showing me more of his family, but I had lost interest. He was wealthy and privileged no matter how you dice it.

Since Sara and Oscar wanted to meet Luca, we stayed longer than we originally planned. Oscar wanted to meet him because he had nothing else to do later, and Sara because she was too fixated on his eye color.

I, on the other hand, made no effort to get out of my chair. There was no need. I was going to quit anyway. I had no intention of sucking up to the new boss like everyone else.

Oscar noticed my discomfort. "Olivia, we can head out now, if you'd like. Sara and I can always meet with Luca another day."

A sudden regret penetrated my heart. "Don't worry, I will wait while you say hello. Plus, it looks like he's free right now."

I watched the two of them walk over to Luca and introduce themselves. I had to remember that even though I was considering leaving BSG, they weren't. Sara still had her wedding bills to pay off and Oscar sent money to his family back in Brazil periodically. BSG was still in their future, though it wasn't in mine, and I had to support them.

What I thought was going to be a quick hello turned out to be a full-on conversation with laughter and jokes. They were really enjoying Luca's company. At one point, Oscar's face was so red with laughter I thought he was going to pee his pants. What were they talking about? Sara turned around and pointed in my direction. Luca's attention followed her finger, and his eyes landed on me.

It happened so fast that I didn't know how to react. I shot up out of my seat, grabbed my work bag and ran straight to the exit door. After being screwed over by my job, I wanted nothing to do with Luca Lontern.

2

I pushed the key into the lock of my one-bedroom apartment, pulled, then turned completely to the left to open. It was a little trick I learned since my landlord refused to replace my door.

Maybe he thought if he replaced my door, it would mismatch the rest of my "vintage" apartment, as it was advertised in the newspaper. After receiving my offer letter at BSG six years ago, it was the first apartment available I could find.

The bright yellow walls and girl boss decor had been staples of my motivation for years. I sluggishly moved into the living room. My bag and car keys slipped out of my fingers and found their way on the floor, not to be picked up until the morning.

I faceplanted into my sofa and the exhaustion fully kicked in. The sofa's velvet material was kind to the skin, and I felt pressured to close my eyes, but the second I did my phone buzzed.

A single notification came up. "One new Message from Sara."

Then, a second. "Two new messages from Sara."

Last, a third. "Three new messages from Sara."

Sara texts in threes no matter the circumstance. The first one is a normal text message. The second one is a further explanation of the first one, regarding what she means and why she says it. The third one is always emojis to soften up the words in her second message.

I had Sara's texting style down to a formula. Though there are some variations of it every now and then, its foundation stayed the same.

Regardless, I didn't want to open it, at least not now. Sara was a traitor for all I know, along with Oscar, who, speaking of the devil, just sent me his first text like clockwork.

They planned it that way. It was silly of me to ignore them since they were only checking on me, as friends should.

I opened the texts messages from Sara:

First message: "Hey, girl, what happened? And why did you run out on us like that?"

Second message: "Okay, I didn't mean it like that. Just checking in on you.

Third message: "🖤🖤🖤"

I moved on from the first message from Oscar and opened it.

Oscar: "Hey, I understand you might not want to talk about it, but I want to let you know I am here for you."

In most cases, I would message them separately, but tonight I didn't have the emotional bandwidth to explain why I did what I did, especially since I didn't know myself.

To Sara and Oscar: "Hey, thanks for checking in. I am okay, just dealing with a lot of emotions right now. See you two tomorrow." Send.

I placed my phone faced down after putting my *Do Not Disturb* on. Were they still texting me? Most likely. Should I text them back? Yes, but I would eventually.

As harmless as Sara and Oscar were, I've been in rare form lately and the last thing I wanted was for them to get the back end of my wrath, so I needed the distance.

My phone buzzed a fourth time, what was it now? I checked to see.

"Incoming Call: Mom," it read.

Weird. She never calls this late.

I clicked accept. "Hello?"

"Hi honey," she said tiredly. "It's been a day."

"What's wrong, Mom? And where is Dad, you two are always on speaker phone together."

"Dad is getting discharged now," she sighed. "He fainted today in the kitchen after feeling dizzy."

I stood up in shock. "Why didn't you call me?"

"You're always busy with work. I didn't want to bother you."

She said something after that, but it wasn't to me. "Thank you, Doctor, yes we'll do it."

"Mom?"

"Sorry, honey," she apologized. "I was talking to the doctor."

"Do you want me to come out tomorrow? Maybe you could use an extra hand?"

"No, I scheduled some follow-up appointments with his doctor this week and we're still waiting for some blood work results. I will keep you updated, love."

"Okay Mom, give Dad a big hug for me."

"Will do."

I hung up the phone and plopped down on the sofa. Today sucked. My eyes wandered to the TV which had been running in the background, but nothing was interesting enough to hold my attention.

I couldn't remember much of what I did for the rest of that night. At some point I dozed off on the sofa, woke up and ate a bowl of off-brand cereal, then moved to my bed. Just as my mind was finally ready to enter a state of unconsciousness, the sudden thought arose, *I needed to set my alarm for the morning.*

With my eyes still closed, I searched for my phone, knocking down several items off my nightstand as a result. When I found it, my eyes peeled open.

"New Message from an unknown number," it read.

New Message: "Hi, sorry to bother you this late. I wanted to make sure everything was okay."

524-739-2930? I don't remember that number.

I hit the keyboard and typed: "Sorry I don't have your number. Who is this?"

My pointer finger hovered above the send button, but I had no intention of pressing it. Instead, I deleted the message. It wasn't the first time I'd gotten weird messages from random numbers, but this was too specific today, and it made me regret deleting it.

● ● ●

My dashboard clock read *8:32*. There were still twenty-eight minutes to kill before the universal nine-to-five shifts started. People called me crazy for getting to work thirty minutes early just to sit in my car. But it was more than just sitting in my car —it was to beat traffic, meditate, and also park in my favorite spot.

There was a nice corner spot under a tree that provided my car with shade during the hot summer afternoons, while its short distance from the building made it an easy dash during cold winter mornings.

I fought the intense urge to open my laptop and start today's tasks. It was an awful habitat of a workaholic, to pre-work before my shift. I don't know when it started—maybe a year or two into working here. The sun would peak over the horizon, and I'd be deep into drafting my fourth schedule email. My colleagues began to question why they were getting tagged on my emails so early. I'd tell them it was because I was a fast typer, which I was, but leaving out the part that I began work an hour ago at my kitchen table.

It was an unhealthy habit that Deirdra confronted me with, concerned that I was not creating a healthy work-life balance. Well, she didn't have to worry anymore. After being dismissed from the director position, I refused to give BSG any more free time. I tossed my laptop in the backseat and scrolled through my phone.

After just a few minutes I was bored with liking people's vacation pictures and baby announcements. Who was I really fooling scrolling through social media? I wasn't that type of person. I cared about things that mattered. I care about getting my work done. I cared about my work laptop, which I probably damaged by throwing it into the backseat.

Just as I reached over to get it, a jet-black Mercedes sped into an empty parking lot, zooming past my car and into the company's indoor VIP parking. Deirdra had many cars, BMW, Roll Royce, Bentley, Porsche, the list goes on. However, the one that had just driven past me was the newest model of Mercedes' coveted and luxurious S-Class. Since I've never seen an S-Class Mercedes in this parking lot before, it must've been a recent purchase for her.

I settled back into the driver's seat, knowing my 2005 Jeep Grand Cherokee had seen better days. My parents gifted it to me after graduating high school. They knew I needed a car for college, and they just recently upgraded my mom's car, so I guess it made financial sense to give me the hand-me-down. However, I was far from getting an S-Class anytime soon.

One by one, cars piled into the parking lot. People slowly opened their car doors with coffee in one hand and a briefcase in the other, all headed in the same direction. I waited until my usual time of 8:47 to finally start heading in.

Once I got inside, I immediately had to adjust myself. There were just too many things in my hands—water bottle, lunch bag, work bag, umbrella, and sweater.

Dale approached me. "Need some help, dear?"

"No need." I stuffed everything into my work bag. "You see?"

"You're a quick woman Ms. Olivia!" he complimented. "Did your mother teach you that?"

I chuckled. "Yes, but she also taught me the bad habit of bringing your entire house with you when going to work," I said, referring to my overpacked bag.

Dale had a unique way of making me smile. He was the employee who didn't want to retire because he loved his job too much. He is, without a doubt, one of the few people I will miss when I leave BSG.

I took out my ID and headed off to the gate. A broad man stood dead set in the middle of the gate. Odd. They don't usually place a security guard there. As I got closer, I quickly realized the broad man was Luca.

Dale approached from behind and read my mind. "Yeah, that Luca fellow is an interesting one."

"What is he doing?" I squinted at him.

"Greeting, I guess." Dale shrugged. "It's his first day, and I already like the fellow. Well, have a wonderful day, Ms. Olivia."

Dale left to return to his duties, but I wish he hadn't. I wished he would walk and talk with me all the way to the gate, through the gate, and to the elevators. That way I have no reason to speak with Luca.

The only good part about this was people flocked to Luca, keeping him distracted. So, maybe I could slip through without being noticed.

Luca was quick with hellos and kept his conversations short. He searched the area, and he made sure to greet as many people as he could before they entered in.

I prepared myself. *Okay Olivia, here we go.*

If only I could weave in and out the maze of people, then I would be safe. He was mid conversation with my colleague, Austin, when he spotted me. His eyes bounced back and forth between Austin and me. Thankfully Austin was a talker and held Luca's attention until I passed the gate.

Several colleagues looked at me strangely after witnessing the theatrics I just performed to dodge Luca.

I ignored the judgement and stepped into the elevator. From a distance, I saw him. His eyes were on me, just me.

What was his problem?

I hurried to press the 'Close Door' button on the elevator, but it wasn't closing fast enough so I kept pressing it again and again, as if it would go faster.

"Are you okay, Olivia?" Ralph, from the finance department, asked. He observed me from the corner of the elevator and was amused by my strange behavior.

"Oh, yeah." I laughed. "I just really need to use the bathroom."

"Ah," he whispered. "My wife gets those too."

I stood there stunned. "You mean, needing to use the bathroom? That's common, Ralph."

He crossed his arm and smirked. "Well, you know why you may need to use the bathroom really badly right?" He ended that sentence with a wink.

I didn't need to continue this pointless conversation any longer, but I was curious about what he was alluding to.

"You still don't get it? C'mon Olivia, you know," he started making letters with his arms.

I squinted my eyes at him, "U?" I asked.

He nodded and started changing his hand position.

"T?"

He nodded and changed position again.

"I," I sighed in annoyance. "Seriously? No, I don't have a UTI, Ralph!"

I walked out of the elevator the second it stopped at my floor. To think that Sara wanted me to date the men here.

Since the day had just begun, people were still walking in, getting coffee, and conversing. Being the department manager, I didn't mind. I actually preferred they get the chit-chat out of the way before the workday began.

I unpacked, turned on my space heater, filled my water bottle, and checked my emails.

One hundred and seven new emails, and I loved seeing them in my inbox. Oscar says I'm a freak for my obsession with emails, but what he doesn't understand is that it's an adrenaline rush for me to see how much I can get done before Sara finds me and pulls me out to lunch.

Knowing I was going to be planted in my seat for a while. I gave a good stretch to my neck and made sure to loosen up my muscles. Now let's see what juicy things we have today.

Yep, just as I suspected most of these I was cc'd in. Boring. Wait, what is this? Why is this flagged? I clicked it open and read:

GOOD MORNING, Olivia,

It was unfortunate that we didn't have the opportunity to meet yesterday. I do apologize as I did not expect the volume of conversations I had. Meeting each and every one of my employees is top of my priority, so I would like to extend a lunch invitation to you. Please let me know at your earliest convenience your availability this afternoon.

Thank you,

Luca Lontern

Director of Operations

Business Solutions Group

ABSOLUTELY NOT! How could I get out of this? My eyes gravitated to the top of the email. Just my luck, it has a read receipt too, so I can't ignore it. I hit Reply and went to work on my keyboard:

GOOD MORNING, Luca,

I appreciate the invitation, as I would love—

Eww. I didn't want to use the word "love", but I needed to sound grateful for the invitation, especially because I planned to decline. So, I kept it and continued:

I appreciate the invitation, as I would love to join you for lunch, but must unfortunately decline. I already have a scheduled lunch with another employee and cannot reschedule. Please accept my apology.

Thank you,

Olivia Kaddel

Consultation Manager

Business Solutions Group

SENT! *Whew*, I leaned back in my chair. Disaster averted, now let's get back to these emails.

"Knock knock." Oscar stood in the entryway of my cubicle with donuts and a frothy beverage.

"Good morning, Olivia," he said, with a crooked smile.

"Good morning, Oscar. Let me guess, that chocolate donut and extra whipped cappuccino are for me."

"Of course," he answered, then passed me my breakfast. "I just want to make sure my overdramatic boss has a delightful Friday morning."

I cringed in my seat as I remembered my abrupt exit yesterday. "Was it really bad?" I held my breath and waited for his answer.

Oscar crossed his arms and gave me the look.

"That would be yes, I assume."

"We just stood there confused," he continued. "Sara and I had just finished telling Luca how freaking awesome you are, and then you just got up and left."

Now I wanted to throw up. "And what did Luca say?"

"Nothing. We said goodbye shortly after that, but seriously, Olivia, what the heck?"

I covered my face with my hands, knowing I messed up. "I'm sorry. I should've done better yesterday. I just—" I stopped, knowing that I was truly sorry but didn't owe him much after that. What I felt yesterday was natural. I could've acted better, but I found my resolve. I was going to quit.

"Yeah, sorry," I finally said. "And, seriously, I really appreciate the breakfast treats. Though, I know it's to cover up the fact that you're twenty minutes late." I shot him the same look he gave me earlier.

Oscar stood up to leave. "Oh, would you look at that? I have meetings, follow-ups, oh and don't forget the presentation we need to go over. Guess I gotta get going."

"Uh-huh, yeah." I took a bite of donut and laughed.

A notification popped up. 'One new message'

Luca: "It's quite all right. I am sure there will be plenty of opportunities in the future, Ms. Kaddel."

Sara will definitely kill me after this one, but at least I didn't have to have lunch with him.

● ● ●

"I am going to kill you!" Sara glared at me. We were at the

water fountain filling our bottles when I told her about the email.

"You're being dramatic."

"No really, I'm going to murder my best friend," she doubled down. "I work so hard day after day trying to land you a date with someone, and something just falls in your lap, and you throw it away."

"First of all, it's not a date, it is a lunch meeting," I clarified, then something triggered in me to turn to her. "Wait. Do you consider work meetings to be lunch dates?"

She puckered her lips and thought. "It has potential."

"You're delusional." I walked away.

She followed while she bickered some more. "Oh, you need a little delusion in your life, that's what makes it exciting."

"Listen, I told him that I was not available to meet for lunch." I shrugged. "It wasn't a lie. We meet for lunch almost every day."

"Yes, but we could've taken a rain check today. Lunch with me is optional."

"Yeah, but he doesn't know that." I smirked.

She huffed. Her high ponytail bounced with every step she took. "Listen, he's not even that bad, and you're going to have to meet him eventually, you can't avoid him forever."

"Long enough until I quit," I mumbled.

"What was that?" she asked, looking up from her phone.

"Nothing." I pressed for the elevator and waited. "Where do you want to go to eat? I don't feel like eating what I brought for lunch."

Before Sara could answer, the elevator opened and there was the very man I hoped to avoid.

Luca leaned against the back railing, hands in his pockets, one foot crossing the other. He lifted his chin and smiled graciously.

"Oh hello, Mr. Lontern," Sara greeted in her high octave voice.

"Hello, Mrs. Beckham," he nodded.

She hurried into the elevator. "C'mon on, Olivia," she mouthed over to me.

I snapped out of it and rushed in just as the doors were closing. We stood shoulder to shoulder with Sara, the giddy one in the middle.

My eyes fastened strictly on the elevator screen, and nothing and no one else. "8...7...6—"

Someone was going to do it. Someone was going to break the awkward silence.

"How was your morning, Mrs. Beckham?"

And it was Luca.

"Glad you asked," Sara clapped excitedly. She was about to let him have it. I just hope she doesn't overshare like she usually does.

"Well, it's a mad house on the sixth floor. Meetings, and circling back, I mean just utter chaos—" I had to nudge her. She got the point. "I mean in a good way, chaos in a good way. We are definitely getting work done," she reaffirmed him.

"Chaos in a good way? I've never heard that before," he pondered. "But you're sure you don't need extra support?"

Don't do it again, Sara. Remember, what I taught you, redirect.

"All under control, but less about me, how was your first official morning?"

Thank God.

He contemplated his answer. "Slow at first but then work started to pick up. I still need to be caught up to speed on where the last director left off."

There was a brief moment of silence. It might've been space for me to ask a follow-up question, but I had no desire to. All I wanted was to run out of this slow elevator.

He bent forward past Sara to look at me. "And your day, Ms. Kaddel? Was it well?"

Now, Sara was nudging me.

"Oh yes," I gave him a single glance to acknowledge him and that's it. That was all he was getting.

"I assume you are off to lunch?" he asked as we walked out of the elevator and into the lobby.

"Yes, would you like to join?" Sara offered.

I shot her a look. She had to be kidding.

This was strike one.

"Would that be okay?" He was looking at her, but the question was for me since I declined him earlier.

"Of course not, I would love for you to join," she answered.

Now she was making me out to be a liar. I already told him no this morning. This was strike two.

Luca still didn't buy it, so instead he turned to me, "And is it okay with you as well, Ms. Kaddel?"

There was no getting out of this one. Sara put me in the corner, and I couldn't say no twice. "It's fine with me."

"Oh perfect," Sara clapped. "There is this nice lunch spot within walking distance. I heard they have great sandwiches and soups. It also—"

Sara's voice fell into the background of my mind. I was too focused on Luca, who had yet to look away from me, even though I answered his question.

We headed out the door, and Sara was still talking, it wasn't even about the restaurant anymore, just random stories about her life, which neither of us asked about.

It felt strange to be in this odd trio. Just yesterday we were critiquing Deirdra's horrible decision in picking him instead of me, and now we were going to have lunch with him. This must've been my punishment for speaking so ill of him yesterday.

We were at the halfway point when Sara stopped in her tracks and held her phone. "I am so sorry," she blurted.

Luca and I stopped, confused by what she had meant. "Is everything okay?"

"I do apologize, but I have a work emergency," she explained.

I caught on immediately. *Oh no. Oh no, no, no, no.* Sara's eyes bounced between me and Luca. With him, a puppy dog expression. With me, sneaky eyes. She had no work emergency.

Luca's tone adjusted when he realized it was just work. "That's unfortunate, but I will not keep you from work."

Sara began walking back while still facing us. "Let me know how the food tastes."

Luca turned around, ready to continue walking while I glared at Sara. She was silently mouthing me all sorts of encouragement.

You go girl!

You got this!

Don't hate me!

Strike three. I am going to murder her. We were both going to murder each other, so I guess whoever gets to the other person first would be victorious.

"Ms. Kaddel, are you coming?" Luca waited patiently at the crosswalk.

"Yes, I am coming."

• • •

Due to overcapacity inside, the waitress sat us in the restaurant's courtyard. It was quite serene, with bamboo sticks and string lights adorning the space. I gazed up at the sky through the restaurant's open skylight. If only it wasn't so cloudy. There was a thirty-five percent chance that rain was upon us.

If needed, there was always a change of clothes back at the

office, but not hair. I had freshly flat-ironed my hair this morning, and any small amount of water will revert it to the curly jungle that it was previously.

"Are you comfortable?" Luca asked abruptly. His voice was still so foreign to me that I flinched and knocked my glass right off the table.

The shards of glass slid across the patio in different directions, silencing the other guests.

The waitress walked over to clean it up.

"Here, let me help." Luca knelt next to her.

"Oh no sir, please sit," she adamantly refused.

"I am already on the floor," he laughed, and he began piling the pieces of glass.

The waitress fought a blush as long as she could before she shouldn't do it anymore. She smiled back at him and even made a joke that they'd make a great cleaning business together.

We're they flirting?!

A custodian came out to finish out the job, and Luca returned to his seat.

"Now, once again, are you comfortable Olivia?" he asked, but this time he moved all the glasses out of my reach.

I couldn't help but glare at him, and he couldn't help but smirk at me.

"Sorry, but I've learned from experience," he hinted at the remaining glass on the floor.

The waitress came back with my new glass. Once she placed the glass down in front of me her attention went only to Luca.

Her hair, which was in a tight bun earlier, was now free from the elastic. She also found enough time to apply a dark shade of lip tint and freshen her cheeks up with blush, somehow all done within the two minutes since she'd left us. It was both impressive and pathetic.

She flipped up her notebook and readied her pen. "What can I get for you today, hon?"

"Wait, I need to make sure my colleague is okay."

His hazel eyes focused on me, this time with a serious face. "I apologize for joking earlier, but you haven't answered my question yet? Are you okay?"

Luca wasn't going to let this go. I'd long forgotten all about the rain, but if I didn't answer him now, I wouldn't ever get back to the office.

"I'm okay, shall we order?"

Luca nodded. "Yes."

The waitress tried again. "What can I get for you?"

"Steak and fries. Medium rare, please," he answered promptly without ever taking his attention off me.

"Oh, that's my favorite. You know how to pick a good one. I'll be right out."

"Excuse me." He stopped her from taking a step. "You forgot about my colleague."

"Oh." She readied her pen but gave no eye contact.

I wanted the steak and fries too, but I didn't want to order the same thing as him.

"Just your house salad, with Caesar dressing."

"Be right out." She hurried away.

Then came the silent part. The part after you order and you have to fill in the wait time with conversation, but usually you'd be sitting across from a person you like. If Sara was here she would tell me to say something cute, funny, something to keep conversation going. But I wasn't like Sara. I was Olivia.

Thankfully, he initiated first. "Did you get my message last night?"

"Message?" I scrolled through my phone, then it hit me. "Is your number 524-739-2930?"

"Yeah." He rubbed his neck shyly. "Sorry, Deirdra gave me

your number in case I had any work-related questions while she was out of town this week."

"Hmm... But the message wasn't work related?" I countered.

"You ran out on me at work, so I'd say differently." He sipped his water casually. "Anyway, you should save my number as well just in case you need anything."

"Highly doubt it," I murmured.

"Huh?"

"Nothing." I saved the number under "Job Stealer" and set aside my phone. "So, why did you refer to me as a colleague earlier? Aren't I your subordinate?"

His eyes grew wide, but only for a split second. It wasn't the type of topic you'd bring up the first time you're meeting someone, especially if that someone was your boss. But I wasn't one for small talk anyway. Since I was already in this dreadful predicament, I might as well pick his mind.

He didn't answer right away and instead grabbed his glass of water and took a sip. Then he leaned back, his cocky grin now in full display.

"What?"

"You want me to refer to you as a subordinate? You're interesting Olivia. Or should I refer to you formally as Ms. Kaddel?"

"Ugh." I twitched. "No, my father used to call my mother that when he knew she was upset with him. It would be a day of 'Ms. Kaddel's' from my dad and 'I am not talking to your father!' from my mom. My brother and I would spend the entire day being the middleman between my parents, all just to hear them making out by the end of the night."

He raised a brow, intrigued. "Oh, didn't see that coming."

I sipped my Chardonnay and nodded. "Yeah, well they never wanted to go to bed angry, so they waited 'til the very last minute to apologize to each other. Anyway, the moral of the story is I don't like to be called 'Ms. Kaddel' unless it can't be helped. It just brings back weird memories."

I glanced up at him, then brought my eyes back down to the table, then to my phone.

Shoot, I thought as I curled in my bottom lip.

He noticed and sat up. "What's wrong?"

My eyes searched the room for our waitress. "Our food hasn't come back yet, and it's nearing one o'clock."

"Yes, but managers do not have timed lunch."

"I know, I just like to get back at the same time my team does."

"Oh you mean, your subordinates."

"My team," I corrected. "I don't call them my subordinates. That would be—" I stopped after realizing the trap he had set for me.

He couldn't help but smile—a nice, wide one too. One that flaunted his pearly whites. He probably gets them whitened semi-annually.

"Well, don't fret. Look." He tipped his head in the direction of the kitchen. "Our food just came out."

Correction: *his* food just came out. A sizzling garlic steak with sea salt fries. The waitress refilled his cup and excused herself.

He kept his hands at his side, making no indication to start eating.

"Just eat, my food is coming."

Luca nodded and started with the steak, though I would've gone for the sea salt fries first. The more Luca cut into the steak, the more sauce oozed out of it. It was the sight of it that made my mouth accumulate saliva.

"You sure you don't want some?" he offered again.

"No, I am craving a cold salad," I lied.

"But your eyes say otherwise," he countered. "Seriously, I don't mind sharing."

I glanced at the kitchen. "It's fine, I am sure my food is on its way."

He wasn't convinced, but he let it go.

"So...do you have any advice for the new guy?"

"Nope."

"Really? BSG's top manager has no knowledge she can give the new director?" He popped a fry in his mouth.

"It's best if you get thrown off the cliff and into the deep end. You'll have to learn how to float if you want to survive."

He stopped eating and scooted in his chair, leaning his elbows against the table, his eyes glued to my face.

"What? Why are you staring at me?"

"You want me to fail."

"I want you to earn."

"There it is." He went back to eating, but it was his casual cockiness that irritated me the most.

"There what is?"

"You think I didn't earn my position," he reiterated as he sawed through his steak, causing the table to tremble.

"You don't have to cut so hard." I held the table still. "Anyway, could you blame me? Your family owns the company. Your birth not only grants you guaranteed employment but also a lifetime of financial security."

"Yes, you're completely right," he admitted. "I have all that and more, but the fact still remains. I earned my job, and for some reason you don't want to acknowledge that."

We managed to keep a reasonable volume despite the tension brewing between us.

I needed to relax, so I forced my mind to focus on something else like where my salad was? Luca was more than halfway done with his meal, but my stomach was curling inside out.

Luca pushed his plate away from him, hinting that he was done and I could pick from him, but I declined out of pure pride.

My stomach did another twist, and if I don't eat now, I will feel it at my desk later.

He excused himself and my eyes followed him to the bathroom. Once the door shut behind him, I immediately went for his fries, lukewarm now but still crispy, then came another and another. I spread the fries around more so he wouldn't notice.

The door creaked open and out came Luca. I swallowed, then immediately wiped my mouth clean of any evidence.

He sat down and observed his plate. "You didn't steal any fries?!"

I solemnly shook my head.

"Really, you're too good then." He frowned. "I thought if I left the table, you would at least help yourself to the fries, especially since you wouldn't accept them when I offer them to you."

The waitress appeared with a colorful garden salad. "Here you go, darling," she said, placing it in front of Luca.

"No, this is unacceptable." The tone of his voice matched the seriousness of his words.

The waitress stepped back, confused. "I'm sorry, sir. I do not understand."

"The salad came late, and it wasn't for me, it was for her." He placed it in front of me. "This is unacceptable, and I am not paying for it."

Several heads swung in our direction—we were becoming a scene.

I leaned over the table and whispered. "It's okay Luca. Let's just leave it alone." Actually, it wasn't okay, but making a big deal wasn't worth the attention we were getting.

A manager stepped out. Luca got up to meet him halfway so I couldn't hear what they were saying. The waitress removed my salad, unsure of what the decision would be. This was so awkward, and we should've just gone back to the office.

Luca came back with the manager.

"Please accept our apologies," the manager said and handed me a to-go-bag. "Your meal today will be on us."

We walked back to the building in silence until he said my name.

"What is it?"

"Tell Sara I give the restaurant a five out of ten. The food was better than the service."

"You know we have Slack for that. I am not a messenger girl, you know."

He ignored the comment and stopped in the middle of the sidewalk.

I turned back to him. "What are you doing? We're almost two hours out of the office. C'mon."

"Listen, I'll quit."

"Wait, what?"

"I will quit," he repeated. "You think I didn't earn this job."

"I mean, I know you didn't," I mumbled.

"Give me ninety days to show you that I earned this job."

I had to be in the twilight zone, some sort of dream.

"I'm serious," he reiterated after seeing that I still didn't believe him.

It made me play around with the idea. "And this is based on my judgement?" I tapped my chin and thought about how many possible ways this could go. "How do you know my judgement won't be skewed? What if I decide out of bitterness?"

He stepped forward, his nose pointed downward, hazel eyes softened. "Because I trust you."

The words caused me to bite my bottom lip. It was a long-term habit I had when I didn't know how to respond to something.

He laughed. "Speechless. huh?'

"Well, it's that you just met me yesterday and you already trust me."

He paused momentarily. He looked at me, but much deeper somehow.

"Is it a deal or not?" His voice became stale.

"You might lose it all. Are you sure about this?" I asked again.

"Well, if it doesn't work, I can always go back to my beach house in Miami and live off my trust fund, right? Seems like a win-win for me."

I gave a deep breath as I readied my final question. "And what are you going to get out of this?"

"That part is for me to know." He left it at that and held out his hand. "So, deal?"

My palm met his and squeezed. "Deal."

3

I pulled into my official unofficial parking spot earlier than usual on Monday morning. It was nearing the end of summer, so I decided to slip on a white dress and wedged sandals as my last hurrah. I straighten my hair over the weekend and completed it with curled ends. Sara would be proud.

Despite it being MMM Day—Monday Meeting Madness—I was in high hopes that today was going to be delightful, especially since it was officially day one of my observation of Luca's performance. On Saturday, I bought a notebook to help me organize my thoughts more clearly. Ninety days from now, I want to give it to him, making sure he understands the reason for my conclusion. I pulled it out of my work bag and inspected its orange and yellow floral design. No one will expect that such a cute notebook would hold the world's most brutal and honest scrutiny of a director.

The clock read 8:05. It was earlier than my usual walk-in time of 8:46, however, due my hectic Monday schedule I found it acceptable for my early arrival. I slipped the notebook back in my bag and headed inside the building.

There was but one other car that occupied the parking lot

other than mine—the black Mercedes S-Class again but parked outside this time. I never knew Deirdra to park her car outside the building's indoor garage, but who knows. She's been in and out of the office at odd times lately.

I reached in my bag for my key card and building keys. Since it was before 8:15 I knew not even Dale would greet me at the door. Thankfully managers were allowed keys, and I didn't have to depend on him if I ever wanted to come in early.

The dark and quiet lobby greeted me. Everything about this place was just so creepy during off hours. Maybe if I hurry to my desk, I'd feel more comfortable. I scanned in at the gate and ran into the elevators.

My finger abused the elevator button, demanding its cooperation. Dale would kill me if he saw this, then he'd reasoned to the jury that it was because I was breaking his poor old elevators.

I tapped my foot repeatedly and looked behind me like I was the last character of a horror movie waiting to be tortured.

"C'mon. C'mon!" My feet readied themself in starting position, and when the door opened I was going to bolt faster than a track star.

It dinged. I took off and rammed right into a firm but warm wall. It happened so fast that I fell backwards, dropping both my work bag and lunch all over the floor.

"Ouch!" My chest throbbed seconds after impact. "What was that?"

When I opened my eyes, there stood Luca in a fitted white button-down and black slacks. He was rubbing his chin and staring down at me.

"Why did you run?!" he said in a heightened voice.

"I—I wanted to—"

"You ran into me!" he interrupted, still stunned by my childish actions.

"I know, I'm sorry."

He bent down so we could be face-to-face. I could smell his toothpaste. He was a Colgate guy. "We both could've gotten hurt!"

"I'm sorry, okay! I'm sorry." I finally got up and shifted my dress back to its flowy state.

My eyes scanned the floor. Everything—and I mean everything—was on the floor. Pens, hair ties, lip balm, ibuprofen, receipts, extra pair of socks, and my sandwich for lunch were scattered everywhere. I bent down to pick up as many things as I could before Luca offered.

Except he didn't ask, he just started on the bobby pins first. Heat rushed to my face, and I avoided his eyes.

"I got it." I grabbed them from his hand. "See," I showed him the floor behind me, "all clean."

"Don't eat that sandwich," he pointed to my bag. "It was poorly wrapped and fell on the floor."

"A few germs won't kill me. Listen, I really just need to head to my desk, I have a lot on the agenda."

"Have a good day." I pressed the 'Open Door' button, ready to retreat from this disaster of a situation.

I took the first step out only to be reminded that we were still on ground level since neither of us requested a floor.

Great. I sighed and stepped back in.

I didn't need to turn to hear the snickering coming from him, but I was determined not to let him get the best of me, especially since my day started so well.

Ding. Eighth Floor. I ran—nope, I walked graciously, out.

"Uh, Olivia," he called. "Is this yours?"

I turned to see every girl's worst nightmare in the hands of Luca Lontern—an ultra-thin leakproof tampon.

I sighed. "Yes, yes it is."

He passed it to me, and that's when I saw it: a creamy brown foundation smudge on the left side of his starched white button down. This is bad.

Luca had yet to realize the humiliation that awaited him throughout the day. Maybe I should just walk away and act like I never saw it—No. I couldn't do it. Sister Catherine, my third-grade teacher, would be turning in her grave.

"Am I free to go now, or do you need to stare at me longer?" he pestered.

"No." I pulled him down the hall and into the men's restroom.

There was wailing of arms, at least on his part. "Wait, what are you doing?"

"Just look." I pointed to the mirror.

Luca turned to see what I meant.

I couldn't bring myself to wait for his reaction, so I went to work, wetting a paper towel with soap and water, and rubbing vigorously against the smudge.

"Last time I try to wear foundation to work," I murmured to myself.

I lifted the towel to see the result. It went from a small brown smudge, to now a medium size wet mark, with a hint of brown.

I sighed, defeated. "Maybe, you can button up your suit jacket? It's our only hope."

Luca laughed. "You know, I have extra shirts in my office."

I crumpled the towel and threw it at him. "Why didn't you say that earlier? You can just change."

He shrugged, "Or I'm just not worried about the stain on my shirt. Have you ever thought about that?"

"That's hard to believe knowing who you're related to. During my first year here, your aunt would send me home to change if she saw even the slightest pen mark on my blouse."

Luca rolled his eyes and leaned in my direction. He was close enough for me to feel his breath but far enough that I wasn't smothered. "Then you will soon see that I am nothing like my aunt. See you at the meeting, Olivia."

• • •

It was nearly eleven o'clock, and I was already behind on my department work. Meetings were eating up my productivity. Most managers spread them out, but I try to get them over with as quickly as I can.

I read the next item on my agenda. "Manager Meeting with Director @ 11 am."

And the other was the CEO meeting with Deirdra at three.

"Olivia, do you need these boxes?" I looked up to see Kerian, the building site manager, standing over me. He's been in and out of the empty office all day asking which things I need and which I don't.

Keiran was nice most days, and the days that he wasn't were because the city's inspector was in the building. On those days, everything that was incorrect in the building was anyone's fault but his own.

"Yeah, just leave them in the corner there. I'll go through them later."

He did as he was told and continued his work in the office. I didn't ask what exactly he was doing as I presumed the office was finally going to be put to use for something else. My guess was another printer room that BSG so desperately needed. I have recommended it several times during department meetings, so it looks like Deirdra finally listened.

My alarm buzzed. It was five minutes to eleven. I took a deep breath and grabbed my insulated water bottle, laptop, and notebook.

"Good luck," Oscar teased from his cubicle.

"Pray for me," I whined and walked over to the staircase.

There was no need to take the elevator. It was only one floor up, and after this morning I didn't need another elevator incident.

I didn't mention it to Oscar, but there was a part of me that was secretly excited to attend this meeting. It would be the first time I could examine Luca closely, and make use of my notebook.

I walked over to the glass doors and pushed. As expected, Luca sat at the nucleus of the round table. A single marble notebook sat in front of him with a BSG ball pin pen parallel to it, and to my surprise, he was still wearing his stained white shirt.

Every seat was filled, with only the seats closest to the door remaining empty. It was only natural that everyone flocked to Luca in his first couple of weeks of being here. Befriending the director was not only a smart move but a career move, and the managers were soaking it up. Connor from Sales brought him a freshly brewed coffee, grande size. Janet from IT had just offered him two tickets to this weekend's basketball game. Her husband, who was the general manager of the stadium, always had extra tickets, though she didn't offer them to just anyone at BSG— only to those she liked. Watching managers fight for Luca's approval was humorous. If they would just do their jobs correctly from the start, they would never need approval—their work would show for it.

I found an empty seat furthest from Lucas' sight line, but it was too late. His eyes found mine, and though he was still in a conversation with Janet, his gaze followed me until I took a seat.

Luca wasn't like the last director at all. Chris always started the meetings the second everyone was seated. Luca waited, seeming to enjoy the countless small talk about weekend recaps and weather. Still, everyone kept an eye on him, trying to get the best read on their new boss.

A fair enough time passed when he finally quieted the room, and all it took was for him to straighten his posture.

He made sure he went around the table and asked everyone how they were doing individually, then corporately. Everyone spoke highly of themselves and even more so when it came to their department.

I couldn't help but snicker under my breath. "Sales were above their quota for the month." "Tech hasn't received a bad review in weeks." Seriously, they have got to be kidding! The number of blatant lies that were spoken was a new record, as far as I could remember.

Luca opened his notebook and wrote after every manager update. Did he actually believe them? Surely. he wasn't this stupid.

I opened my floral notebook and jotted down a single note:

-Lacks Discernment?

I'll leave the question mark there to give him time to prove me wrong, but until then, it will be a mark against him.

"And last, Manager Olivia for the consultation department." Luca searched for me. "There you are," he said, bending himself to try to see me.

"How has the consultation department been since your last meeting with Chris?" He readied his pen.

"We've maintained our client database for the last quarter, however—"

Luca put up his finger requesting me stop. "I'm sorry, I can't hear you well and I also can't see you." He got up and pulled out his chair. "Here, can you come sit in my seat?"

His seat? All heads swung in my direction giving me death stares. If looks can kill, I'd be unrecognizable.

"I don't bite," Luca assured. The rest of the managers awaited my answer.

What was he trying to do, win me over? But the faster I sat in his seat the faster we would continue.

I picked up my laptop and notebook and squeezed myself

behind my colleagues. "Excuse me. Sorry," I said as they grunted and scooted in their chairs. It was only a ten-foot walk, but it felt like a walk of shame.

Once I sat down, I resumed my update. "So, my department is quite busy. We have some presentations to new clients in the coming weeks, our existing clients also are asking for extra services regarding quarter's financials. We're definitely all hands on deck."

He crossed his arms and twisted his mouth, asking questions at a rapid fire speed. "How is your department that busy? Is the team getting work done on time? And why are your clients asking for more services? Are the services you're providing not enough for what they need?"

Seriously?! He didn't ask any of the other managers follow up questions. Why was he picking on me? The other managers whispered to one another.

"Look who's getting in trouble now."

"Good thing we didn't get drilled."

This was not time to lose focus. I straighten my posture and answer him firmly. "My team is a well oil machine. Our work is done on time and we stand at ninety four percent client satisfaction rate. Our numbers don't lie, and if you still don't believe me you're more than welcome to fact check on the master file."

Luca nodded as he registered everything I said. Once I finished, he didn't ask for his seat back. Instead, he walked around the room as he spoke about what he looks forward to in his new role as Director.

There was no PowerPoint. No agenda. Just walking around and talking. My chair, along with the other managers' chairs, turned 360 degrees several times to give him our undivided attention. I felt nauseous by the end of it. I reached out to sip on my water bottle.

"Thanks for sitting tight through this," he concluded with a grin. "Before I let you go, I just want to inform you that since I like to be an engaged manager, I feel as though my main office is too far away from the action, and I'm better suited on the eighth floor with the Consulting Department.

What!

The flow of water that had been soothing my throat came to an abrupt stop at the end of his sentence, causing me to choke.

Luca sped over and bent down. "Are you okay, Olivia?" He angled himself to get a better look at me.

Others asked how I was doing but weren't as attentive as Luca. All the attention was getting to me and making me even more flustered.

I cleared my throat. "I am good." The words rushed out of me. "Just went down the wrong pipe."

Luca stood up but didn't walk away. Instead, he stood behind me and finished. "So, moving forward I will be in the spare office on the eighth floor alongside the consultation department. Thank you for your time in this meeting, we'll hold one-on-one meetings in following weeks so please look out for my email.

• • •

It was nearing time for my next meeting, and being that it was with Deirdra, it probably could go either way. I stood in the bathroom and stared at myself under the intense fluorescent lights.

You can do this Oliva. You can do this.

I took the elevator to the top floor, and Abby, Deirdra's new assistant, chatted blissfully on her phone, barely acknowledging my arrival, let alone making eye contact.

"Hello," I greeted.

"Huh? Uh, yeah give me one moment." She put the phone down and looked up. "Can I help you?" she asked sharply.

"Uh, yes, Deirdra and I are supposed to have a meeting today."

She scrolled through her computer, her eyes moving side to side as she read. "Nope, don't see you."

I took a deep breath before responding. "Check the red tab."

"How do you know—"

"Because I created it for Deirdra's last assistant." I responded. "Just check—you'll see what I'm saying.

She gave her mouse two clicks and then there was an "Oh."

I couldn't help but roll my eyes. Abby was a piece of work, but it made sense. She was a desperate hire from a friend of Deirdra's. Back when I was hired, the interview process was both in phases and strenuous, but apparently that doesn't apply to friends' or family's children who need a job.

On my way to her door, I could hear voices laughing from inside, causing me to slow down. Was Deirdra currently in a meeting? She had to be; there were two voices.

"I know I made the right choice. BSG will be in good hands," I heard her say.

"Thanks Aunt Deirdra. I think you have a good plan here and I'm excited for the future."

Aunt? So, it was Luca. He's the only person in the building for whom it was acceptable to call Deirdra *aunt*. Why was he here? I grunted in despair.

"What was that? Hello?" Deirdra called out. She heard me. "Olivia, is that you?"

I pushed open the door to expose myself. "Good afternoon."

"Oh, perfect, I have both of you," she said, clapping. She pointed to the chair next to Luca. "Please sit."

I sat down and turned to acknowledge Luca.

He leaned into his seat, his left arm slouched over the side. What was his deal?

Deirdra cleared her throat, breaking the tension between us. "Thank you both for coming."

Deirdra never started off a meeting by thanking me for coming, so already I knew something had to be off.

Her attention bounced between Luca and me. "Olivia, I am so happy to have Luca join the BSG family. He'll be a wonderful addition to what I hope to grow in the future. Now, I will be short as I know you two will have plenty to do." She rotated her laptop to face us, showing us her screen.

"At the end of the quarter, we have our yearly board meeting. This year, I would like to prepare a presentation for our board members."

The words *board members* shot down my spine. Sure, I saw a few of them at our annual Christmas party, but I've never been considered to meet with them on a professional level.

"Looks like I grabbed both of your attention." Deirdra smiled as she observed our change in our demeanor. "So, we as the company have seen exceeding growth in the last two years, and with that growth, members are concerned about losing the company's objective as more personalities join the group. I would like you ease their concerns with a presentation of what BSG will look like moving forward. The meeting will be held three months from now. This is a great opportunity for—"

I accept," Luca said strongly. He was now sitting on the edge of the chair with straight posture. "It will make the perfect confirmation to my future here." He winked at me from the side.

"Perfect!" she beamed. "We—"

"I accept too." There was no way I wasn't going to lose to Sir Luca. This was a no-brainer. Presenting to the members will not only expand my skillset, but prove to Deirdra how wrong she was about picking Luca as the new director. Yes, this was Luca's family business, but I was more skilled and versed in the business than he was. Not only that, but the meeting would also mark the end of the quarter, marking the end of our deal on Luca's performance. For once, it was as if stars were aligned for my comeback.

"Wow, thank you for accepting! I am so excited for this collaboration."

"Collaboration?!"

"Yes dear, surely I wasn't going to pick between you two." She got up to get her water from her desk.

"Yet, you pick him for director," I mumbled under my breath.

He snickered.

She came back to us. "So, three months from now sounds like a fair amount of time to prepare. Now, do we all agree on collaborating?"

"Yes." He nodded.

Deirdra silently nodded before turning to me, "And you, Olivia?"

Despite the secret agreement between Luca and me, Deirdra and I had our own beef to squash. She uses my free time to benefit the company. She has been the cause of my anxiety attacks for the last six years. I am her go-to person for everything work and non-work related. And for what? All to advance her nephew above her hardest working employee.

"Olivia, dear." She whistled at me. "Are you listening? Do you accept?"

I hate when she whistles at me.

"Yes, I—" I cleared my throat. "—we'll deliver an exceptional presentation for the board members."

She clapped in excitement, "Delightful. This is wonderful. Just so wonderful."

● ● ●

"Are you staying late again?" Oscar asked at the entryway of my cubicle, his satchel across his body and his blazer hanging in hand.

"Yeah, the meetings took longer than expected so I am catching up on a few things for tomorrow." I studied him closer. He had a slight smile across his face, but he refused to make it any more evident.

"Let me guess, you've got a date. That's the fifth one this month."

"Yes, but get this—it's with the same person," he announced happily. "Anyway, sorry I can't stay with you tonight."

I glanced at the work that needed to be done. It's beneficial to have a second person knock out the tasks with me but tonight wasn't that night.

"Don't worry about it, I'll find a way to get it all done." I shrugged.

"It's not the work I am concerned about. It's that I don't think you should be here alone."

"There has to be another manager working late tonight," I reassured him.

Oscar snorted. "As if. Olivia, no one stays late on a Monday. Oh wait—" he tiptoed above my cubicle to get a better look. "Luca is still here." He said, relieved, and looked down. "Don't give me that face, Olivia, just be glad someone is here."

"Or you could please reschedule your date," I pouted.

"Nope." He laughed. "Now, go and make friends with your new roommate. See ya."

Some time had passed, and I walked out of my cubicle to see what Luca was doing. He was at his desk, the stain from earlier was worse, his tie was nowhere in sight, and his hair had lost its uniformity. The afternoon must've beaten him up. He looked like a first-year attorney who'd just lost his first case.

A sudden nudge in me urged me to go in and ask how he was doing.

No, Olivia. What are you doing? He is the director. Surely he knew what the job entailed when his favorite aunt handed it to him on a silver platter.

I turned around to walk away. It took only one step until I heard my name. *Damn.*

"Olivia," he spoke. His voice was much softer than before, still deep, but less authoritative.

"Yes," I walked in. A tower of boxes stood lopsided in the corner. Two new leather chairs stood across his desk. The walls were naked, and shelves were unoccupied. There was no personality to this office, not even desk trinkets.

Maybe he was some sort of minimalist, though that wasn't something I could write in my notebook as a mark against him.

"Are you done judging me?" he inquired.

"I am not—"

"You are," he smirked, "Don't worry I don't mind." He walked to the front of his desk, leaning against its wooden frame. "Judge away."

He was definitely six two. I tilted my chin to almost ninety degrees to spot the widest grin that boasted very white teeth.

My attention drifted to his eyes which were, as hard as it was to admit, so much softer up close. I was never a blue-eyed girl, but I'd be a liar if I said hazel eyes were never a thing for me.

"Olivia," he spoke in a lowered voice, a sweeter voice. "It's time to come back to me."

My eyes released him, and I took a seat in his guest chair. "Umm... your office looks nice," I fibbed.

"Really?" He did a 360 to confirm. "Your expression says differently." He returned to his seat. "But thank you for stopping in. I did want to apologize."

"Huh?"

"I moved in without asking," he clarified.

"Yeah, but you're the boss, so who am I to say otherwise? You can do whatever you want."

He tilted his head and looked at me strangely.

"Did I say something wrong?"

"No." He shrugged. "You're just... interesting."

Interesting left a bad taste in my mouth. It brought me back to my sophomore year crush. Tanned skin, dark hair, not the top student but top five pick for the football team. Alec Bavtech. He wasn't what all the girls my age were searching for, which gave me a great advantage. I remember after being partnered with him for chem lab, I was certain he'd fall for me. I worked hard to earn his affection. Turns out, he talked badly about me in front of his friends, saying I was weird and unattractive. When I confronted him about it, he neither confirmed nor denied the accusation. Instead he said what he meant to tell his friend was that I was "interesting" to have a lab partner, and that I should find someone as interesting as me to date.

"Did I offend you?" Luca asked.

"More like triggered, but that's not your fault."

Luca frowned, but I needed him to stop reading me, so I changed the subject.

"Where are your diplomas?" I pointed to the empty wall. "So many accomplishments need to be affirmed with accreditation."

"I don't want them on the wall," he said with a twitch.

Did I just touch a nerve? I shifted my position on the chair. I contemplated asking for a follow-up but decided it would be for another time.

"Anyway, welcome to the eighth floor." I stood up to leave. "Make yourself at home."

"Wait," he stood up, "I'll walk you out."

I laughed. "Walk me out? It's unnecessary, I do this all the time."

But Luca had already followed me out of the office with his coat and briefcase in hand. "No worries, I'm heading out too."

I sighed and stopped at my cubicle to collect my things. If I prepared fast enough Luca wouldn't have time to investigate my cubicle and—too late. He was eyeing the pictures of me during my graduation, then the pictures of my mom and dad when they were first dating back when bell bottoms were a thing, then (of course) me and my brother dressed up for the Christmas pageant at our church when I was eight.

"I'm ready." I quickly positioned myself at the door. He followed me out, but it bothered me how quiet he was, especially after seeing my personal pictures.

The walk back to my car was cooler than normal for September evening. I wrapped my cardigan around my body while stealing a glance at Luca.

The temperature didn't bother him; in fact, he took his suit jacket and offered it to me.

"Oh umm, I—" My words struggled to find the right order. I took a deep breath. "No thank you."

"I don't stink," he blurted. "I mean I don't think I do," he sniffed himself.

I stared at him, shocked by how transparent he was with his body odor. The entire thing made me relax from my intense shivering.

"No, it's just that my car is up ahead." I pointed to the tired Jeep sleeping underneath the tree.

His eyes squinted at the questionable machine I called my car. It was at that moment that the small dings and rusted rims felt more prominent than they had been before. His hand slid across the patches of discoloration on my hood, and I couldn't help it anymore.

"Ugh, just say it!" I blurted.

His eyes zoomed in on me, his face blank. "Excuse me?"

"Why don't you just say it already? Say what's on your mind. Tell me that my car sucks." I readied myself for his criticism.

He withdrew his hand and stepped back. "Actually, no, that's not what I was thinking."

"Oh, tell me then."

"No," he said flatly. "Not until you start telling me what's on your mind about me. You don't get access to what I think about you."

I stood there without a thought on how to respond.

"See you tomorrow, roomie." He waved goodbye and disappeared into the darkness.

4

The transition into fall was seamless, but I was so occupied with work that I hadn't noticed I'd traded my favorite wedge sandals for boots and my summer blouses for fuzzy cardigans. I thought it was a style upgrade, but Sara said otherwise. I didn't argue with her, with all the work I'd been juggling between the presentation and running my department, there was no time for shopping.

I opened my laptop to an empty agenda, something I haven't come across for months. Maybe I made a mistake? I flipped open my calendar to make sure—nope, nothing.

Now I needed to fill my day with something. My thoughts went to the pending presentation. I did as much as I could alone, but I was now at the part where Luca and I needed to join forces and put it together. My stomach turned with nausea at the very thought of it.

I'd dodged most interactions with Luca for weeks now. My secret: only communicate via email despite him working across the room from me.

It also might've helped that he's been inundated by coming up to speed with his new position. Mountains of paperwork occupied his desk, with little progress being made due to his other responsibilities.

There were several nights that I left late, but I always made a point to peek over Luca's office. Sure enough, he was there with papers in one hand and navigating his computer with the other. He always looked the same past five: rolled up sleeves, loosened shirt buttons, and tired eyes. One night, a small urge to ask him if he needed help emerged within me. It wasn't foreign to my character; I simply love helping others with various tasks, needs, or goals. Watching Luca struggle night after night, triggered compassion in me, but I needed to murder that compassion.

Luca Lontern was born into enough wealth and resources to succeed and have a healthy and satisfying life. While he didn't deserve a lack of compassion, I withheld mine because he never had to struggle the way I did. Our lives will never be equal, so at least I'll let him get a taste of what I must do every single day.

Oscar popped his head. "Psst, do you want to—Are you okay? You look upset."

"Really?" I relaxed my expression. "Sorry about that."

"Do you want to know the current tea this morning on the CDG? I am sure it will distract you."

CDG stood for *Consultants Department Group Chat,* an exclusive group chat for employees of my department minus me because I'm a manager. Of course, this was a private chat due to the volume of gossip it entails. Every department had its own, and the thread was more active than all of the manager's inboxes combined. There were plenty of days that I missed being part of it, especially when I was kindly kicked out the day I was promoted to manager, but I understood it was a necessary protocol. Thankfully, I still had Oscar as my faithful informant.

"Let me guess, Is it about Luca?"

"Uh-huh." He nodded and leaned over the divider. "I know you were less than pleased when he moved into the empty office, but look at this way, at least they have no reason to talk about you anymore. All eyes are on him."

"Jeez, thanks I guess."

He winked at me and descended back down.

I turned back to my screen to see one New Message from Deirdra.

OLIVIA,

Could we do a check-in at eleven a.m.? It will be short. I apologize in advance for inconveniencing you.

-Deirdra.

ELEVEN A.M.? I looked down on the screen. That was in four minutes. I hated last-minute meetings. I picked up my notepad and headed for the elevator, taking long, deep breaths on the way up. I needed to remember that despite the presentation and my job description, I no longer wanted to give Deirdra any extra energy or headspace in my life. She might not take it well, but she was going to have to get used to it.

I hurried down the hall and stopped at Abby's desk. You'd think my chunky booties would make enough noise to peel Abby's eyes from her phone, but you'd be wrong. Her constant swipes from left to right told me she was an hour deep into social media, and if I didn't say something now I'd stay here until the end of the hour.

"Ahem," I signaled to her.

Her eyes ventured up to me but slowly returned to the phone after a second. "Oh hey, Olivia. Do you have an appointment? Deirdra won't see you if you don't have an appointment."

"I do have an appointment. At eleven."

She put her phone down to check her computer. "You aren't on Deirdra's calendar, nor on the red tab folder."

I checked the time and it was 10:59. "Well, it was a last-minute meeting. Deirdra just emailed me."

"I'll wait for Deirdra to email me then," she said and went back to her swiping.

You've got to be kidding me. Abby was never the best assistant, but now she was just plain rude.

"Could you just check?" I asked. "Listen, if Deirdra reprimands you, just blame it on me."

Abby grumbled underneath her breath, but she finally checked.

She returned seconds later and avoided eye contact with me. "Okay, you can go."

Immediately Deirdra stood up to greet me. It was so fast, it was as if she was sitting on a pile of hot coals. Despite the cool weather she had on her favorite white Saint Laurent dress. Her freshly-dyed blonde hair was pinned up in a 1950s bun while three curly pieces dangled above her eyes.

"Good morning, Olivia." She grabbed my hands and gently squeezed them. "I am so happy you were able to make it."

Her abnormal gesture caught me off guard, but I regrouped myself to give her a proper response. "Of course," I lied.

"That's good, because I just wanted to let you know that you have always been an outstanding employee at BSG. My grandfather, bless his heart, would've been proud that you are part of his company."

I gave her a simple nod, but I didn't want to talk about her or her family's legacy. So, I changed the subject.

"Umm, are you taking a trip soon? You always wear Saint Laurent when you're flying."

Her eyes ventured over to her suitcase in the corner. She must be leaving straight from work.

"Yes, Greece again, but for nine days this time. I'll be reachable, but only through email. I will also send a manager memo of everything that needs attention while I am away."

"Understood. I will be on the lookout for it this afternoon." I stood up to leave.

"However, that's not the reason why I called you in," she interrupted.

"Oh?" I returned to my seat.

"So, I know it's last-minute, but there is an upcoming business conference this weekend that I cannot attend due to my trip. It's invite-only from a lovely couple that I've known for years. It's imperative that BSG is represented at the conference—not because we need the networking, but because the hosts are dear friends of mine and I don't want to let them down. Would you be able to attend the conference on my behalf?"

Unlike before, I didn't answer with a quick "yes" or "of course." Not because I couldn't make it, but because I wanted to make her sweat a little. Cruel? Maybe. Do I care? No.

She scooted to the edge of her seat. "Is something wrong?" she frowned.

I crossed my legs. "I'm certain there are other candidates that are better suited for the opportunity—Brenda, Jackson, Lamina, I mean I guess anyone could do it."

She sighed. "Yes, but Brenda is not as charismatic, Lamina is still new to the company, Jackson is not up to date with technology, and every other manager has something they need to excel at before I send them on a work trip of this nature. Listen, you're the best one suited for the opportunity."

Maybe I just needed to hear those words pass her lips for me to finally say, "Fine, I'll go." And sure enough I did.

"Perfect." She perked up. "Thank you. Thank you, Thank you a billion." She leaned back on her chair. "You don't know how much you've saved my butt."

It was odd seeing my ruthless boss in a fashion of mercy. She never begged me for anything, probably because I'd always said "yes" before she could beg, but even so, I'd never seen her so grateful. Deirdra is too rich to beg and too prideful to be grateful. I couldn't help but theorize.

"Great, I'll book you the best hotel suite, the best room service, everything. You're set to leave tomorrow morning."

"Tomorrow morning? So, soon?"

Deirdra typed away on her computer but still managed to balance her attention on me. "Yes, but don't worry, any work that you have will be postponed till after the weekend or given to Oscar. I don't want you to be overwhelmed on this trip."

"Got it." I stood up ready to leave, then stopped. "Will you be notifying Luca of my absence or should I?"

"Don't worry about Luca, he's scheduled to attend the conference with you."

• • •

I kept my attention on my spaghetti and avoided Sara and James's stare from across the table. It was several hours past my meeting with Deirdra and Sara invited me to dinner with her and James in their new apartment downtown.

"So?" Sara's voice heightened.

"What?" I finally looked up to see a very tense Sara, and very confused James.

She rolled her sky-blue eyes. "Don't 'what' me, Olivia!? You're going on a trip with Luca. Your life has become a romance novel!" She brightened in excitement.

James tapped her on the shoulders. "Honey, Olivia is far from happy. You can see it in her face. She dreads this."

I can always count on James to bring Sara back to reality. When I met James, my impression of him was another finance guy who would be in my life for approximately six months—the usual time frame in which Sara would be occupied with a man —but something about James kept Sara coming back for more.

Sara folded her arms and reclined back in her chair. I wasn't giving her much.

"Well at least you're bringing some stylish clothes," she said, pointing to the pile of dresses hanging over the sofa. Earlier, Sara handpicked some of the most memorable pieces she stored in her wardrobe. "They haven't seen the light of day in ages, so you're doing me a favor," she insisted. "Do you need anything else?"

"No, Deirdra gave me her card if I needed anything else. Just have to save the receipts and not go over 7k."

"Wow, you must be doing Deirdra a big favor," James said.

He wasn't wrong. It dawned on me this afternoon that Deirdra was going above and beyond to make me comfortable this weekend. What else she had going on, she didn't tell me.

"Anyway, wish me luck this weekend. Luca is going to pick me up at eight for a four-hour car ride."

Sara almost choked. "He's picking you up to ride with him for four hours!" She turned to James. "Okay, that's it, there is no need to watch my rom-com tonight. Olivia just gave me my nightly dose within one conversation."

I pushed in my chair and reached out for my plate. Her hand stopped me.

"Don't worry, James has dish duty tonight. Plus, you have to go home and practice your makeup. You're a quick learner, so just watch one or two makeup tutorials, and make sure your lips are plumped and ready." She puckered her lips to emphasize her point.

"That's my cue to leave." I stood up and slipped on my sweater. "Thanks, James, for dinner. Next time, dinner is at my place." I headed to the door, but Sara followed.

"Oh, take a joke, Olivia." She laughed. She grabbed my work bag from the closet and handed it over to me.

"You, of all people, do not joke about romance."

"Fair." She leaned against the door frame and watched me slip on my boots. "And I know how uncomfortable it must be to sit next to a person who took your dream job. It sucks."

"Thank you for finally seeing that." I hugged her. "As excited as you are for me, this is a very bitter trip in my perspective."

"But..." She puckered her lips at me once more.

"Oh, no!" I let go of her and walked to the elevator.

"Listen, all I'm saying is to enjoy yourself this weekend. You never know." Her voice was amplified in the hallway. "Hope you hit lots of traffic."

5

Maybe I should've tried harder on my makeup this morning. I moved closer to the mirror to inspect my artistry—a faint blush paired with a sleek cat eye and darkened brows. The simple makeup seemed suitable for a four-hour car ride where only one person could judge: Luca.

I sighed as I looked deeper at the heavy bags underneath my eyes. Staying up late did me no justice, but my hair desperately needed to be straightened. There was no way in hell that I was going to fight with my curls for three mornings straight. I finished the look with a slicked back bun, leggings, and a faded Tahoe sweatshirt.

The outfit should be comfortable enough for the car ride, plus I needed comfy clothes to combat my stomach cramps which started up this morning. My doctor said it might be linked to greasy foods or stress due to uncomfortable situations. Being that I was about to sit in a car for four hours with Luca, both greasy foods and uncomfortable situations were likely to occur.

My phone vibrated across my nightstand. "Job Stealer," it said. Here we go.

I cleared my throat of any raspiness before answering, but how I should answer was another question. "Good morning," "Hello," "Hey," what type of greeting should I use to start off a three-day work trip with my boss?

"Olivia? Olivia? Are you there?"

Oh! I held the phone against my ear. "Morning. No! Sorry, I meant to say "good" before that. Like good morning, you know." I slapped my forehead. This was getting off to a bad start. I needed to shut up.

"Good morning, yeah, I've heard of 'good morning' before." He laughed. "I'm outside waiting for you. Ready when you are."

Wait, he was already here? I rushed over to the window and peeked out my blinds. Sure enough, a jet-black G wagon was parked against my curb. Luca leaned against it, in a plaid button down paired with navy blue jeans, Nike Air Maxes, and a baseball cap.

I let go of the blinds and turned around. "Okay, I'm coming."

"Did you have to make sure it was truly me before confirming that you were coming?"

Damn, he saw me. How do I play it off?

I placed the phone on speaker and gathered the last of my things. "Oh please, I just didn't think you'd pick me up this early. We agreed on eight, not 7:39."

"Yeah, sorry about that. I wanted to get a head start on the road since we're leaving during the thick of rush hour." His tone softened—he really was sorry. "Anyway, take your time, Olivia."

Something about how he said that made me smile. "Take my time, you say? Okay. I will take my time."

"Not too much time, otherwise I'll have to come and get you."

"You don't have a key!"

"But I know how to pick locks," he argued.

"Tssk, where did you learn that from? Boarding school?"

"I'll tell you once you come out of that apartment of yours. But seriously, we do need to get on the road soon."

"Okay, I will be right out." I hung up the phone. Seven minutes and forty-six seconds. What the hell! Why am I talking to my boss for almost eight minutes about non-related work things? I snapped out of it and did my last-minute chores.

When I finally came outside, Luca was nowhere to be found, just a black G-wagon. I rolled my suitcase over to it and looked through the tinted windows. He wasn't in the car either. Where could he have gone?

Voices prompted me to turn left, where I found Luca chatting with my neighbor Neil. Since the day I moved in, Neil was a grumpy retired firefighter who I'd never seen crack a smile, not even when I told him that I found his lost dog. Not until today, that is.

Luca sensed me and turned around. He smiled, but it wasn't his usual smile. It was one I'd never seen before. It was an ear-to-ear smile that caused his eyes to squint and his cheeks to flush. For a second I forgot he was my boss, and I stared a little too long in his direction before finally breaking eye contact.

He jogged over to me. "Are you ready?"

"Yeah." I cleared my throat and recomposed myself. "I see you met Neil." I tilted my head in his direction. Neil continued to look at his car, while making subtle glances at us out of his own curiosity.

"Yeah, you know that's a 1982 C3 Corvette?" He pointed at Neil's car. "He keeps it in mint condition too. Olivia, those cars are collectables, I mean they're just beautiful." The more he talked about it the more excited he got.

I didn't interrupt, simply because I had nothing to add. Neil had that car wrapped up six days a week, all except for Saturday between the hours of 10:00 a.m. and noon, when he washed and waxed it. Due to his callous personality, I opted to admire the Corvette from a small sliver of visibility behind my blinds. Just saying hello to me took him fourteen months of me living here, while it took a random stranger named Luca a mere five minutes.

"So, he offered me a glance at his engine, "Do you want to come check it out? It'll only be a few."

I held my breath as the thought of finally coming close to an American Classic was only a head nod away, but it was short-lived once I remember the only reason I was allowed to go near the car was because the Luca was allowed first.

"No, I'll wait here."

His excitement dropped a little. "Oh, okay, let me get you settled in then." He walked over to the passenger side of the SUV and held it open. "Come in."

I got in, but with hesitancy. "Thanks, but next time I don't need the chivalry."

"It's in my blood, sorry." He closed the door before I could make a comeback. It didn't stop me from saying it behind the glass window.

"What?" his yelled was muffled by glass, as he pointed to his ear "I can't hear you! Let me check out the engine then we'll go!"

He is such a liar. He is a job stealer and a liar. I settled in and waited. At least he gave me the privacy to snoop inside his car. He was definitely a Mercedes guy. It was more than just the sleek interior. It was the two-tone premium leather seats, screen displays, and modern day technology, a car that lived up to its six-figure price.

Wait, was it this? I picked up a white paper bag from the center compartment which read "Olivia". Next to it sat a large, iced coffee with a medium dark coffee. He got me breakfast?

The car door opened, and I flung my back to the seat and

instantly grabbed my phone. I didn't need him to know that I was snooping.

"Okay, sorry about that." He tossed his cap in the backseat along with his button down. "Wait, did I scare you?"

"No," I lied.

He smirked. "Sure," he said, then mumbled something.

"What?" I turned to him.

"Nothing." He shrugged and stretched out his arm behind my chair, holding it for stability as he put the car in reverse.

Knowing the girl in me wanted to study his physique, I fought the urge to turn his direction, and instead I pinned my eyes to the windshield.

He moved his hand back. "Did I make you uncomfortable?"

"Of course not. It's just that you have a brand-new car with a backup camera, yet you still turn around."

"Silly, isn't it?" He blushed. "It's a habit of mine, I guess. However, this car isn't new, about three years old. I just don't drive it often."

"Right, you prefer the c-class."

"That's not the reason. I actually prefer this car. It's a big car." He rubbed the wheel. "Kinda like yours."

"How dare you compare my 2000's Jeep to this beauty we currently sit in. Have you gone mad?"

"But your Jeep has memories, I can tell," he countered. "Anyway, I want to use this car more, but's it just me. So, there's no reason to."

Sensing the quiet, he peeked over in my direction, the corners of his mouth itching upwards. "Umm, made you breakfast." He handed me the bag.

I received it and peeked inside to see a lukewarm egg and bacon croissant. "Thank you," I put the croissant back in the bag and figured I'd wait till we parked at a rest stop to eat it.

He sensed my hesitation. "You can eat in the car, I don't care about the mess."

"Is this to make amends for picking on me during meetings, because you're going to have to make hundreds of croissant sandwiches to scratch the surface of forgiveness."

He laughed, "Just eat, I worked really hard on it."

I unwrapped it and took the first bite, warm cheddar cheese instantly melting into my taste buds followed by hints of salty bacon.

I couldn't resist and closed my eyes to savor every bite. Once I finished, I tossed the wrapper in the bag, folded it up, and wiped my hand with the last sanitizing wipe I found at the bottom of my purse.

Luca eased the car to a full stop at a traffic light. He rubbed his hands together and turned to me with eager hazel eyes and the brightest smile. "So, what's my grade?"

"Huh?"

"Wait, you still don't believe that I made it?!" he tilted his head.

I scratched my head and thought about how I could answer honestly.

"I'm not saying that you aren't capable of making delicious food, but you don't give me chef vibes, that's all."

"Oh," he pressed on the accelerator, and the car merged effortlessly from the road onto the endless interstate. "You're going to be in for a weekend of surprises then."

The first hour was dry. I scrolled on my phone but managed to conjure up closed-ended questions. He answered, and then out of formality he'd asked me "What about you?" I'd answer, then return to my phone until I'd find another question to ask.

This continued until he finally stopped at a gas station. He parked the car but kept his hands on the steering wheel and his eyes ahead.

"Are you okay?"

"Olivia, don't ask me questions unless you really want to know." He got out and pumped gas.

I put my phone away and wondered if he was truly annoyed.

We continued the car ride without conversation, and surprisingly it wasn't bad. Later he requested that I choose a radio station, I agreed and opted for a Hispanic one. At the midway point Luca asked if he could connect his music, reasoning that it was absolute torture to listen to salsa music while having a seatbelt on.

I agreed, and we were soon met with an iconic 1970s playlist. Luca made sure to hit every beat with his imaginary sticks and drums while navigating driving. He even passed me the imaginary mic during the choruses, many of which I did decline.

So, he sang by himself, and though he was off-pitch, it didn't bother him at all, nor did the truck drivers giving us dirty looks.

The whole thing was quite comical, despite me being a grump.

We stopped to grab Taco Bell upon my request, and it was also an excuse to give him a break from driving. Though I regretted it an hour later.

We were twenty miles from the retreat before my gut began to revolt. I covered my stomach with my purse, hoping to buffer the noise. Luca had long turned off the music, but I desperately needed the background sound.

I reached over to the volume knob, but I was too late. In the four years since I've had my condition, my stomach has never sounded so vicious until today.

"Owww!" I held onto the pitch, and immediately Luca turned to me with unwavering concern.

"Oliva, are you okay?"

Before I could answer, he swerved the car into the shoulder lane ignoring the honking cars behind us.

Once the car was parked, he held my seat with his hand to get a better look at me. His hazel eyes were now adamant in not letting me go.

"It's fine I just—Ugh." My stomach successfully trapped a pocket of gas, and a sharp pain engulfed my left side. This episode had been the worst I've ever felt, and there was no way of hiding it.

"Ouch. Ouch." My body had curled itself into a ball as I waited for the pain to subside. When it did, I opened my eyes to see Luca hovering above.

He was in utter silence. His hand kept him steadily against my chair while his other hand held his weight against the dashboard.

"Olivia," he said, using his authoritative voice. "Look at me."

I did. He was neither angry nor upset, two emotions I was sure I would meet. Instead, his eyes managed to tread between the fine line of soft but serious.

"Yes, Luca?" The words had come so naturally to me it sounded like a whisper.

He inched closer, dismissing the car console that had been our fence for the duration of the car ride.

"Talk to me," he whispered back.

"It's—", my mouth froze.

For years, I've locked my personal matters away from prowling colleagues, successfully letting them only go as far as to Sara and Oscar. Yet, for some reason, just a moment ago, my tongue was readied to let loose at the request of Luca.

"I'm okay. It's just discomfort."

He sighed, knowing that's all he was going to get, "You know, you double blink when you lie," he said casually.

"Huh?"

He slowly moved back to his seat. "About two times before the lie, and then a lip bite after the lie.

He shifted the car into drive and merged back onto the road. I released my bottom lip from my teeth and smoothed it over with my fingers. *When did I start biting my bottom lip?*

Luca watched me from the corner of his eyes. "You didn't know about it, huh?"

The tension between us had become awkward, and neither of us knew how to recover from the exchange.

"I'd guess it's a good thing for me," he continued. "I'll know when you lie to me at work." He turned to me to make sure I saw the wink.

I responded with an eye roll, glad to know we were back to regular tempo.

• • •

"All done." I laid out my eight outfits on the king-sized bed. This should be adequate for a two-day, three-night conference. We arrived two hours ago and parted respectively to our separate suites.

In reality, we were both exhausted after the long car ride and needed to recharge before the evening cocktail session. All I remember is coming in and passing out on the bed. I would've napped longer if I didn't have to practice my makeup. After a steamy shower, I sprawled out my newly purchased makeup across the desk.

I closed my eyes and took a long, deep breath as I coached myself.

Okay, Olivia, you can do this. You watched hours of makeup tutorials last night on YouTube. You learn quickly. You! Can! Do! This!

Well I did it, sort of. One hour just to get my eyeliner, brows, and lipstick just right. Yep, for one hour I could've done so many other impacting things for the world, but I chose to enhance my face.

I opened my phone to see the overwhelming pile of messages I had from Sara.

Sara: Hey, have you arrived yet?

Sara: Sorry, I just miss you. Update me.

Sara: 🖤🖤🖤

Me: Hey, the car ride wasn't as bad as I thought. Also, fun fact Luca loves to sing, and by the way, I did my makeup."

It should've been enough to keep her occupied. It wasn't. It took mere seconds before three dots blinked across my screen.

Sara: "Picture or it never happened."

I snapped a quick photo to send to her and then silenced my phone. No matter what her verdict was, I wasn't going to change my makeup—there simply wasn't time. I'll save the contour and highlighter for tomorrow's activities.

I finished the look off with a royal blue midi dress, orange wedges, and freshly tightened bun.

Okay, time check. I ran over to my phone. *1 New Message from Luca.*

Luca: "We should walk in together. Coming in a few."

His message was three minutes ago, meaning he's probably walking over now.

I twirled in front of the mirror. *Damn, I looked great.* The royal blue slimmed me down, while the velvet dress gave me texture. I was unsure about the pop of orange at first, but it tied it together perfectly.

All I needed was chandelier earrings, and I—

Knock. Knock.

Great. I grabbed my earrings and a purse. After this morning, I wasn't going to have Luca wait on me again.

Oh wait and perfume.

Knock, knock.

"Coming!"

I grabbed the perfume my cousin bought me from France

two years ago and sprayed just as my mother taught me, neck, wrist and between the legs twice.

Knock. Knock.

"All right, all right I'm opening it." I ran over, almost tripping over my suitcase, but I caught myself and reached for the doorknob.

We stared at each other—it was inevitable.

My eyes went from the top down, starting with his freshly-washed hair. He had got it cut recently, I hadn't noticed it in the car, but the top was the perfect amount of messy transitioning into sharp faded sides.

He finished his look with navy blue suit brown loafers. Sleek, masculine, expensive.

"Did I pass?" he finally asked.

"Huh?" I returned my attention to him.

"Do I look good enough to walk with you?" He clarified before doing a 360.

He had to be joking. All the women in the office drool over him, while the men envy him. If he needs a confidence booster, he can go ask some other girl.

"No, we match too much. You should've done a tan suit." I closed the door behind me and walked around him to the elevator.

He caught up once the elevator door opened. It was packed with people. According to the front desk receptionist, the hotel was hosting two other conferences that weekend. Luca managed to find us some room, though I would've waited for the next elevator if we weren't late already. I took a deep breath and joined him.

A group of men dominated the area, spreading their legs to maximize their space as they joked about their recent golf trip. The few women kept to the side, clearly frustrated by the inconsideration, but contributed to the tight space by holding large shopping bags. The woman beside me eyed me in irritation, most likely at the fact that I fit myself into the already-packed elevator. She whispered something to her friend, after noticing that I was with Luca. They chuckled as they whispered more.

The moment brought me back to my high school era, a vicious time when girls laughed at other girls for the various high school drama. I was usually the girl being laughed at, so it was nothing unfamiliar. I can only thank God that I moved past that chapter in my life. I just wished that the memories stayed in the past, too.

Luca's warm arm snaked behind my back, gently pulling me away from them and closer to him, leaving me taken back by our sudden closeness.

"We're almost out," he whispered. His eyes scanned the elevator, but they were fiercer then before. A few men glanced back at him but said nothing and vice versa. Sara said that was a guy thing, talking with their eyes instead of their mouth.

I wondered what they were saying.

The elevator dinged once it arrived in the lobby. All at once they rushed out, pushing each other in the process.

Luca held me tighter as we both waited to get out last. Once it was empty, we walked out but he pulled me aside.

"Are you okay?"

"Yeah," I nodded. "Are you?" I asked, referring to his uneven breathing and tense forehead.

"Yes," he took a needed breath. "Anyway, I just want to warn you about what you may encounter at this party."

"Huh? You mean sort of what I just experienced in the elevator?"

He nodded. "Yes, could be worse, could be better, but I suggest you stay close to me for the remainder of the night."

Usually, I like to handle my own affairs, but I was in enemy territory with only a twenty-dollar Marshall's clutch in my hand.

These high-end parties weren't my specialty, and I knew that, so I obliged him.

Through the glass door swam a sea of business executives; women were in elegant colors and name brand heels. Their entire outfits would probably cost me a month's paycheck, plus overtime. The men were dressed in suits similar to Luca, and of course they wore the trendy suave loafers.

An urge of uneasiness arose in the pit of my stomach. Suddenly my velvet dress was not good enough for an event of this nature, and my orange wedges were too bright for an evening cocktail.

I held my body as if I could cover it from the judging eyes. I slowed down. Luca noticed, his attention went straight to my stomach. He wanted to ask the question again, the one from the car ride earlier.

He opened the door, and all eyes were on us. When Deirdra mentioned how highly anticipated the company's representatives were, she wasn't lying. Groups of people flocked to us, pinning us to one side of the room. They seemed to know Luca immediately, congratulating him on his new position and his move to the area.

"We have to do lunch sometime soon, Mr. Lontern."

"How was your summer in Oxford?"

"Have you ever met my daughter? Oh, she is lovely. I do believe you two are around the same age."

These were the people who booked vacations ten times a year, the ones who had multiple addresses and trust funds in their name before they were born.

Wealthy, prestigious, and unrelatable.

Again, I wanted to retreat. No one would notice anyway. I was just as worthless as a server with an empty cocktail tray to these people. But any effort to escape would be followed by Luca's death stare and a waist tug back to him.

The last pull kept me glued to his side, so I gave up and abandoned my escape plan. At this point, the only thing I was excited about was seeing Alice and Kenneth, Deirdra's friends, but they too were preoccupied with conversations.

The night was coming to a close as the servers slowed their service and people held on to the last of their wine glasses.

Luca was finishing up his chat with the cofounder from X Technologies, Henry Tablet. Henry had dominated the conversation with pointless mentions of his golf tournament awards and newly purchased yacht. He was so intrigued with himself that he hadn't realized Luca had lost interest and had been an auto pilot.

"Would you like to join me one day Mr. Lontern? The seas are quite a sight during cooler evenings."

Luca hesitated. He was distracted by the hosts, Alice and Kenneth, who made their way over to the mics. He probably thought it was his way out of giving Henry an answer, but Henry was adamant about getting something out of the conversation.

"Umm," Henry said confused.

I stepped in. "I do apologize, Henry. Luca and I work closely together on projects, and I believe we are booked for the upcoming weekends. He'll get back to you."

Henry walked away unsatisfied.

"Luca," I nudged him.

"Yes, Olivia?" Luca turned to give me his full attention.

"Oh, so you are capable of responding." I crossed my arms like a displeased mother.

He scoffed. "I don't want to go on a boat ride with him."

"Understandable, but you didn't have to ignore him."

Luca soften his expression "I didn't want to answer him, but next time I will since I see you don't like that."

I don't know why the last part of his sentence made me

blush, so I tried to brush it off. "I mean, you don't have to listen to me. It was just a suggestion and all."

"Good evening." Kenneth's voice echoed through the garden's hidden sound system.

I gave my attention to Kenneth, but Luca was a lot slower to follow suit. He wasn't finished with our exchange. His eyes lingered on me for a while longer.

The speech was short and graceful. Kenneth and Alice explained that they wanted us to be well-rested for tomorrow's agenda; therefore the night would come to a conclusion.

The disappointed guests exited the room, whispering each of their theories on why the cocktail event ended early.

The common theory among them was that Kenneth and Alice ran out of money for booze and needed to save whatever was left for the rest of the conference.

So, this is what the rich talk about, I thought to myself. What a shallow thing to say.

We were almost in the elevator when one of the guests ran up to us, clearly wanting Luca's attention.

I stepped back, giving them some privacy.

"Hey, um Luca, you know, me and the guys are going to the pub in town. Did you want to come along?" I heard him say.

"Thanks for the invite, but I—" He looked back at me.

"Girls are invited too," he added seeing that I was Luca's obstacle.

"No." His answer startled both of us by how quick it was. He clearly felt bad and tried to adjust. "I apologize, but I'll pass tonight. Thanks for the offer."

The elevator door opened, and his hand pressed against the small of my back and guided me in.

"Have a good night," he said, bidding farewell to the man.

Unlike before, it was an empty and peaceful elevator ride up —a familiar scenario; just me, Luca, and the soft melody of jazz music. The music was too tempting, and I couldn't help but sway side to side to its rhythm. From the corner of my eye, Luca watched me and maybe even judged me, but I didn't care, not even a bit. I was in my happy place.

The elevator dinged at my floor and Luca walked out while I danced out with the music still playing blissfully in my mind. It wasn't like me at all, and maybe it was the alcohol. If Sara was here, her mouth would've dropped wide open at how comfortable I was, but there was only Luca to witness my abnormal behavior. He, too, was amazed by my ability to dance around him until we reached my door.

The hallway was empty—everyone made after party plans except us, but at least Luca had been invited somewhere. There was no reason why both of us needed a lonely night.

I stopped dancing and felt dizzy instantly. However, I wasn't drunk enough to fall on Luca, though I knew Sara would've died to witness that moment. I opted for the wall. My body thumped loudly against the drywall.

"Ouch," I held my side.

"Olivia," he spoke and reached out for me. "Take it easy."

"I am okay, I got it." I struggled to find my footing.

He completely ignored me and helped me up anyway. My hands rested against his chest, while I safely stood straight against the front of his body. His left hand wrapped itself across my lower back and secured me in place. I had yet to look up at his eyes, which I knew could be the death of me, especially after the interactions we've been having.

Once I snapped out of it, I stepped away.

"I'm sorry," he blurted. "That was out of line. I uh—"

"You should've gone to the pub. It seemed like fun," I interrupted. "Plus, just because we came here together doesn't mean you have to decline an invitation because I am not invited."

"I know I just—I want—" Luca was having a difficult time with his words.

It reminded me of my five-year-old niece, stumbling over her words whenever she couldn't make sense of what she was feeling. Luca wasn't a five-year-old girl, but it still gave me a soft spot for him.

"It's okay, Luca." I unlocked my suite and waved to him. "Goodnight."

"Goodnight, Olivia," he smiled back.

6

Despite it not being a regular workday, my body naturally woke up at seven a.m. After saying goodnight to Luca, I couldn't remember much of what I did after, except that I was watching some drama from one of the seven channels that my TV provided.

I stretched out to feel for my phone under the mountains of blankets and satin pillows. Once I felt the small metal device touch the tip of my fingertips, I clutched it and looked at the screen. My eyes took a second to adjust to the LED light, but a plethora of messages had piled up since last night. Most of which were from Sara, who requested an in-depth review of my Friday ventures. There was also a message from Oscar, who joked that the department wasn't the same without my authoritarian leadership—at least I hoped it was a joke. The last was a message from Luca, sent just after midnight.

Luca: Hey! Forgot to mention, Kenneth and Alice would like to have breakfast with us at nine a.m. See you then.

He left no room for a "yes" or "no" response, meaning it was part of our job. Breakfast was in two hours. One of those hours would be dedicated to my hair and makeup alone, meaning I needed to start now.

I slid out of bed and fell face-forward onto the floor. My first instinct was to wallow in my misery of being here, but there was no time, so I decided to save my wallowing for my shower.

Eight thirty-seven and I just finished gliding my peach lip gloss over my lips. After slipping on a yellow midi, I curled my hair into soft waves, and slipped on blue flats. I snapped a photo and sent it to Sara.

Olivia: I think I'm getting better. Call you after breakfast. *Send.*

I grabbed my clutch and headed out the door. Suite 901. I knocked and waited. No answer. Maybe he was busy and I should've met him downstairs, or maybe he went out to the pub and had someone in the room. In the midst of walking away the door swung open. He stood tiredly in the doorway in plaid pajama pants and a white tank top. His hair was matted, and dark circles surrounded his eyes.

"Olivia, I didn't set my alarm. I'm sorry," he apologized.

We had but twenty-five minutes before our meeting with Kenneth and Alice, both of whom Deirdra had emphasized to not disappoint. As much as I would've been excited to jot this strike down in my cheetah notebook, I was far from that mindset and in recovery mode.

I grabbed his arm and pulled him inside. "We've got twenty-five minutes to make you look convincingly put together, not freshly rolled out of bed."

Luca hopped in the shower while I grabbed the ironing board. I told him he had five minutes to smell like a bar of soap. The hardest part was picking out his clothes. I stood at the opening of his closet where an assortment of suits, shirts, and pants hung before me. It was hard enough to pick out clothes for myself, but now I had to pick a coordinated outfit for my boss.

I snapped a picture and sent it to Sara.

Olivia: What should Luca wear?

Six seconds later:

Sara: WHY ARE YOU IN HIS ROOM!?

INCOMING CALL: SARA

I sent it to voicemail. There was no time to chat.

Message 2: Sara: AHHHHHHH! You better call me after breakfast!!

There was nothing after that. Great, she was so obsessed with the fact that I was in Luca's room that she disregarded my cry for help. I tapped my pointer against my lips and thought.

What would Luca look good in? In all honesty, he looked good in everything. When you carry the attractive gene, you never have to try hard.

My eyes wandered to the crisp white T-shirts I wish he could wear again, but I knew it was too casual for the occasion. There was, however, a pale yellow button down, maybe with those blue slacks from yesterday, plus the brown loafers in the corner. I spread the outfit on the bed to make sure it worked and surprisingly it did.

The slacks just needed a quick iron, and they would be good to go. The shower made an abrupt stop, hinting at me that I needed to be quick.

I was almost done when the door slid open followed by a cloud of steam and a half-covered Luca.

Iron, Oliva! Look at the iron! I coached myself.

"So, I—uh—picked out your clothes."

Luca held the toothbrush in his mouth while he held the shirt for inspection.

Curious to see what he thought, I quickly glanced at him then turned back to the iron.

He left to spit out the toothpaste and then came back with a cocky grin.

"So, just to be clear, you were lying yesterday when you said that it doesn't look good when we match, because clearly we match again."

Matching yellow and blue? I glanced in the mirror at my yellow dress and blue flats. How could I spin this around? I bit my lip and thought.

"Well, I think matching is more fitting for a morning breakfast. We look like a team now." I passed him his pressed slacks and observed his expression.

We were toe-to-toe, though he had almost a foot over me. My nose pointed up, his nose pointed down. The smell of cedar aftershave lingered around his smooth chin, mixed with the scent of minty toothpaste that oozed from his mouth.

He broke the stare and laughed. "Like I said before, I know when you're lying so you can let go of your lips."

I loosened my lips from my teeth. "Anyway, let's just go. We're going to be late."

He shot me a look and smirked "Do you mind hanging out in the living room so I can change into my matching outfit?"

"Oh, uh, sorry." I grabbed my belongings and hurried into the living area.

He came out just a few minutes later, not as sharp as he usually was but good enough for breakfast.

I walked in front. He walked closely behind with a right hand in his pocket.

In passing, we recognized some of the attendees from last night, most of whom looked hungover from late night activities but still managed to greet us.

Kenneth and Alice waved hello from a private room with a round table. I gulped, not really knowing what to expect. If yesterday's encounters were a sample of what Kenneth and Alice were like, then I already knew it was going to be less than enjoyable.

"Ahh, Luca." Kenneth stood up and gave him a kiss on each cheek. "You look well." He patted him on his arm and gave him a good look, "And strong."

"And you must be Olivia?" Alice asked. Alice was a short woman deep in her sixties, dressed in fine silk. She managed to form a smile with her thin ruby lips and reached over to me. "Nice to meet you. Please sit."

Luca apologized for our lateness on his behalf, but Alice told us not to worry about it and that they were just grateful we agreed to have breakfast with them.

The majority of the conversation was between Kenneth and Luca, with occasional remarks by Alice.

There were stories about past family trips to Dubai, tournaments, and Cambridge reunions. Being that there was nothing I could add, I kept to myself and focused on my Eggs Benedict.

Alice looked my way and nudged Kenneth, whispering something to him, but it was too low for me to hear.

"Olivia, forgive me," he scratched his head. "I haven't seen Luca for almost a decade, and I wanted to catch up, but that doesn't excuse my behavior. Please don't think I was ignoring you."

I wasn't expecting to speak, so I quickly swallowed and dabbed my mouth with a napkin. There wasn't much I knew about Kenneth and Alice. I don't even know if we had anything in common. Regardless, I was here to represent Deirdra, so I did just that.

"That's quite all right," I answered. "I'm honored that you welcomed me to your convention on behalf of Deirdra, and I know how much she wanted to be here this weekend."

Kenneth laughed. "Oh, Olivia, when we're around you don't have to talk Deirdra up so highly. We've known her since she was in grade school and have mentored her ever since. We know she can be a you-know-what," he winked.

Alice nudged him. "Kenneth! A handful is what my husband is trying to say," she corrected. "However, Deirdra is getting better, honey. We must give her that. Especially with Luca and Olivia running BSG, Deirdra will have nothing to worry about."

• • •

I sat down at the station provided for us. It was nearing five p.m. and we had just finished the bulk of the convention. There were a total of five speakers, a breakout session, and a Q&A. Thankfully, Luca and I were only here on the basis of a long-standing friendship, so not much was required of us, but others had to set up booths to network.

"Here you go." Luca passed me a water bottle.

I took the bottle and examined its structure. "A glass bottle for water?"

"Imported from Italy," he corrected. "Though I'm sure the water from the water fountain down the hall is just as good, and could've saved them a ton of money."

I snorted.

"What?!" He sipped, his eyes still on me.

"Nothing, I just didn't expect that coming from you, that's all."

He tilted his head and stared at me longer. He opened his mouth to respond but moved on instead.

"Well…" He leaned back. "We're done on our end."

"Aye, Luca," a deep voice called out.

We looked around hoping to find its owner. It didn't take long before a stocky man walked over to us. His hair was a color I'd never forget—crimson red. The type of red that women would spend hours at the salon trying to achieve.

When Luca spotted the man, they slapped hands then pulled in for a typical bro hug.

"Someone's been hitting the gym." He patted Luca's arm.

"Yeah, but I am never going to catch up to you."

I gave the two some space and snuck away while they weren't looking. After so many encounters during the convention, I'd come to one conclusion: these people don't care to talk to me. They don't care to network with me or anything else. Outside of my career, I am not part of their world. I was an outsider.

I weaved through the clumps of people until a voice called me by name.

"Olivia."

No one knew my name here except for Luca, and he had a signature way of saying it, but that wasn't him.

"Oliva, I'm here."

I turned to see Kenneth waving at me. He had been in a group of two older men chatting. Immediately, the men glared at me. I stole Kenneth's attention away from them.

Slowly, I approached but chose to stay outside the circle.

"Hello." I smiled.

"Ahh, darling." He kissed me on both sides of the cheek. "What a day! Have you enjoyed yourself, my love?"

"They were definitely some memorable moments," I admitted. "The trip was unexpected, but I've enjoyed stepping away from the office."

"Kenneth," the other man said, "Would you care to join us outside?"

"No, I'm quite exhausted by the topic, but feel free to continue without me," he hooked my arm with his and walked us the opposite direction.

If we weren't at a convention, people would've mistaken me for his caregiver given how tightly he was holding on to me.

"Ahh my darling, when you've been in the business as long as I have, you're able to recognize the suck-ups and frauds."

Having no idea where his statement came from, my only

conclusion was that it pertained to the gentlemen he'd parted ways from.

We walked and did a loop around the hall, and to my surprise, everyone waved at us.

Kenneth waved back and called out. "Thanks for coming." Then he pointed to me. "And this is Olivia Kaddel from the Business Solution Group."

It continued until he turned to me "Olivia?"

"Yes?"

"This room is filled with high-ranking individuals, but they are not without flaws. Now, I don't know you personally, but Deirdra has mentioned you many times in the past. One day she mentioned you so many times, I told her that I have to meet you before I die."

"Really?" I asked in utter disbelief. "Deirdra spoke about me?"

"She has, and something tells me that you'll exceed in whatever you do. You're an intelligent young woman who will one day make a name for herself in the business. Don't forget that."

My heart moved at such a compliment—I've never received such praise like that, especially from someone with his reputation.

"And also," he stopped and turned to face me. "BSG is a wonderful company that has launched you into your career, but at the end of the day, always do what's best for yourself."

"Sure, but wouldn't Deirdra get mad that you're telling me this?"

"I've always told Deirdra the same thing. Do what's best for her, whether it has to do with BSG or not."

Now I was really laughing. "Sir, Deirdra *is* BSG. That's all she knows. It's been her only job since she was a teenager. To be honest, I couldn't picture BSG without her."

He didn't say much after that, just nodded and smiled.

"Well, my love, this is the end of our journey for the evening, as I do believe that Luca wants you back." He pointed to Luca, who was watching us alongside his friend.

I grabbed his cold and wrinkly hand and gave a gentle squeeze. "Thank you again for everything, Kenneth. I will definitely keep your words in mind."

"Hey."

"Hey." Luca stepped forward. "I was looking for you. Sean invited us out."

Sean reached out his hand. "First, let me introduce myself. I'm Sean, a good friend of Luca's. We've known each other since we were kids, but I'll leave all the boring stuff out since I'm sure you had enough of that this weekend. Anyway, do you want to come with us to a local pub tonight?"

Sean was sweet to include me in the invitation. However, I wanted to be honest with him since I had no interest in taking another pity invite.

"Thanks, but I'm sure that you and Luca need to catch up, and I don't want to be the tag-along."

"Tag along?" Sean playfully nudged Luca aside. "Listen, I know enough about this guy. Plus, he talked about you most of the conversation, so I had to meet you for myself."

"He talked about me?" I amusingly crossed my arms.

"Yeah, and it will only be the three of us, away from this crowd," he said, referring to the guests.

"Sure. Let's go."

• • •

Dark and wooden, it was exactly what every pub looked like and no different from the one I went to in my twenties.

Sean suggested one at the edge of town where he hoped

none of the conference attendees would drive too. Regardless, it was a Saturday night and the room was packed.

The young host found a standing table in the back.She slapped down three menus on the high table. "Sorry, I had to put you near the bathrooms. That's all we had."

"Aye Luca, this brings back college memories," Sean said, then leaned over to me. "You know, Olivia, your boss was always the responsible one, I was actually the crazy one, so it's only fitting that he became a director before I did."

"I mean, I had to manage a group of four drunk friends including myself. Someone had to be responsible," Luca corrected.

A skinny waitress with a messy bun walked over to us. She was young, a sophomore in college if I had to guess, who had too many layers of foundation caked on her face and overdrawn lips. Her attention immediately went to Sean and Luca, but specifically Luca, who she leaned into.

"I've never seen y'all around here. You must be from that hotel convention downtown."

"Uh, yeah," Sean answered. "Something like that." He kept the small talk short.

Her question was directed at Luca, but since Sean answered, she now stepped closer to him.

"Well, I hope to hear more about it as the night continues." She pressed her chest closer to him.

"Yeah, can we put in our orders?" Sean asked bluntly. "It's been a long day."

"Yes, what can I get for y'all?" Her accent didn't match our location at all, but neither of us were interested enough to ask.

We ordered two Guinness and a gin and tonic. I thought it was enough, but then Sean added another round of Guinness for the table.

She wrote very slowly and looked up frequently, squeezing

in as many non-related questions as she could. When she finally left, a heavy sigh of relief was felt around the table.

I crossed my arms. "I blame that on you two, had it been only me I would've had my drink in my hand already."

Sean laughed. "Hey! Her eyes were on Luca; don't look at me. Just like back in the day, women would never leave us alone with this guy around."

"Oh, I've seen it before," I agreed, remembering my first time with him at the restaurant.

Our drinks came rather quickly despite our waitress attempting to prolong service. Sean was for sure a veteran drinker—he took gulps at a time while Luca took sips every now and then before setting it back down. Sean finished the Guinness so quickly he went in for his second, within minutes.

"Easy," Luca warned. "We're not in our twenties anymore."

"Sorry." He placed the drink glass down. "I just wanted to get buzzed enough so Olivia could tell us how the convention is an example of how people can be so out of touch and shallow at the same time."

"Something like that," I said. I meant to elaborate, but a line of girls heading to the bathroom nudged me aside. This was the second time people almost bumped into me. Not only were we near the bathrooms, but I specifically was in a bad spot.

"You good, bro?" Sean asked Luca.

Luca glared at the guests coming in and out of the bathroom.

"They don't need to push." He scooted over. "Olivia, move closer to me, that way you won't get hit."

I heeded and moved closer to him, enough for bathroom clearance while still giving him elbow room.

My drink was decent enough to finish but not enough to order a second, which in hindsight was best, especially with my low tolerance to alcohol. I had only drunk to the halfway point when my body started to feel it. Surprisingly, I managed a coherent conversation with Sean. He wasn't half-bad as the convention's other guest. I learned that he had been living in San Francisco for six years, where he works and partly owns a successful start-up company with a friend. He and Luca had known each other for twenty-two years, but their families had known each other for longer. He also likes to play pickleball over the traditional wealthy sport of golf.

"Enough about me, what about you? How did Olivia get to where she is today?"

"It's not because it was handed to me, that's for sure," I couldn't help but say.

"Ouch," Luca held his arm as if he'd been shot.

Sean studied both of us "Am I missing something?"

Before I could answer, he had already answered for me.

"Well, you're not wrong, more than half of the convention's attendees were handed their opportunities."

I raised a brow at his assumption "Only half?

"Yeah, believe it or not, the other half still needs to perform exceptionally to get a spot at the table."

"Hmm, sure." I sipped my drink.

Seeing that I was dead set on my stance, he eventually let it go and moved on to various stories of he and Luca being wild and crazy in their earlier years. Despite my dislike for the typical wealthy bro-hood of men. I was entertained by their wild adventures. Sean was a great storyteller and would always end it with "We'll have to take you there next time, Olivia."

Sean was the crazy drunk who made you feel like family.

"Ouch." I held onto the table to keep my balance. Another man ran to the bathroom with his hand over his mouth, followed by his buddy.

"Uh oh," I heard Sean say to Luca.

Before I could turn around to see what they were talking about, a firmed hand wrapped around my arm. Luca tugged and

I obeyed. I moved in closer, and in doing so I got too close and elbowed him hard in the gut.

"Oh, so sorry." My hand rubbed that spot that I had just assaulted.

He bent down to meet my ear. "Don't worry about it. Are you okay?"

"Yeah," I nodded, "but I hit you pretty hard."

"It's fine, I probably deserved it," he joked and handed me my drink, but it took longer for his attention to stray from me.

"Ahem," Sean coughed. "I'm still here."

"Sorry man," Luca lifted his glass with his left hand while securing me with his right hand from the passing guest. For some reason, it worked. His hand took most of the hits, but he didn't seem to mind. Maybe because he was having a deep conversation with Sean, whom he was still catching up with. The rest of the night was the typical bar scene; loud voices, swanky waitresses, unruly men, and yet I didn't mind.

Every so often, Luca smoothed over my bruised arm in a circular motion. When I looked up at him, he was still in conversation with Sean, oblivious that he'd been rubbing my arm. Sean saw and laughed at his friend's inattentiveness.

"What? Am I missing something?" Luca finally asked, catching on.

I guess it was an opportunity for me to tell him to stop rubbing my arm and pulling me closer, but for some selfish reason-—no, not selfishness—-but maybe a way of compensation for stealing my dream job, I decided to let it happen.

"Nothing." I smiled and leaned closer.

7

Saturday Morning with no obligations feels like a crime in your thirties. I couldn't remember how long I stayed awake staring at the hotel ceiling, but I guess it didn't matter. The convention was over, and the only obligation today was to head back home. Once I was ready to get up, I showered and washed my hair. I dressed in light washed jeans, a cropped t-shirt, and tennis shoes. I would've slipped on a baseball cap, but my curls were never this bouncy after my normal showers at home. So, I slipped the cap back into my suitcase and closed it.

That was the last of everything that needed to go back in the bag. I rolled my suitcase into the hallway but stopped halfway out the door. *Oh wait! The bed. No matter what, I always leave something, and it's always underneath the bed.*

I ran back to the bed, knelt, and searched with the flashlight on my phone. A long wire stretched across the floor. How did my phone charger get there, and how am I going to get it out? It was so far in, I had to stretch but only my fingers could brush the cord.

After three tries, my body was midway under the bed, but I finally grabbed it. "Yes, I got it!"

"Olivia?" I heard.

Great. Luca was greeted by his employee inexplicably halfway underneath her bed with only her butt and legs visible.

I shuffled my way out and stood up to face him, curly strands falling in front of my eyes. I moved it away and hoped it didn't catch any dust bunnies on the way out.

"Morning, Luca. I hope you slept well."

His face twisted in amusement. "I did, thanks for asking. How did your charger get all the way underneath—" he stopped. "You know what, never mind. What you do in your room is your business." He smirked and turned around to get my suitcase.

"Hey!" I followed him down the hall. "You know I don't do weird stuff in my room. What am I supposed to do with a phone charger anyway?"

"Listen, I don't judge."

"Then what's with the rolling of the eyes," I accused.

"Huh? Did I roll my eyes?"

There was no point responding; he was having too much fun teasing me and it was barely ten a.m. A few people from the convention caught us leaving. They waved goodbye, but didn't bother to chat as they, too, were exhausted from the weekend activities.

Valet already had the car pulled up in front, heated and with complimentary coffee to-go in the cup holders.

"Ready?" Luca fastened his seatbelt.

"Yep." I sipped my coffee and smiled.

"You're happy this morning," he noted, putting the car in drive. "What do I have to do to make you this happy at work?"

The question was interesting enough to think about, especially since I couldn't remember the last time I'd been genuinely happy.

Luca stopped at a light and took a moment to glance in my direction, his eyes narrowing as he studied me. "You got an answer yet? And you can't say to give you my position because those are not the terms of our agreement."

His question was harmless, but it got me thinking. So, I turned to him, the guy whose eyes glowed even on the sunniest October day.

"I don't know why I'm happy," I admitted. "Maybe it's because I'm not stressed from work, or because it's the weekend."

"Or maybe because you don't have to be around shallow people any longer," he suggested.

"Possibly." But even after I considered it, it still didn't sound right. I stared out the window and sighed. "It's beautiful today; too bad we'll be traveling for most of it."

"Hmm." His attention turned back to the road. "Let's stop somewhere, then."

"Somewhere?" The thought excited me much more than it should have, coming from someone who was dreading a trip with her boss in the first place. I cleared my throat to flatten my tone. "Ahem, so where were you thinking of?"

"I don't know. Do you mind checking around?"

I opened my phone, but it lasted three seconds until it died. I forgot to charge it last night, not that I would've known where the charger was anyway.

Luca noticed. "Here, use my phone," he offered.

I scrolled through Google. "There's a scenic spot...but it's an hour in the opposite direction... Oh, how about this local theatre? But it's reservation only. Wait there's a..nope, it's closed on weekends. Ugh!" I moaned and slumped further down in my seat.

Luca did his best to be involved despite having to drive as well. "What's wrong, Olivia?"

"Nothing, I just can't find anything. I wish I knew we were going to stop somewhere earlier, that way I could've planned."

"That's what you're frustrated about." He laughed. "Let's wait a bit. There might be more options the further we drive."

There were, in fact, no more options. If anything, our options decreased the further we drove.

"You're such a liar." I poked at him. "There is nothing to do and we've been on the road for a couple of hours now."

"It's been an enjoyable couple of hours, has it not?" Luca countered. "We stopped at the smoothie spot, you took over as car DJ, and you finished our road trip snack in twenty minutes."

"What!" I held up the empty bag. "Sunflower seeds are addicting, especially the ranch flavor."

"If there's an apocalypse coming and I'm with you, I'm definitely taking over food rations, otherwise we won't last a day."

Just as my mouth readied itself for a slick comeback, Luca's phone buzzed in my hand. It was the third time in the last hour.

"Hey, do you want to pull over so you can take that? I can step out if you'd like."

"Step out on the side of the road so I can take a call? No." Luca refused, "It's just my cousin, Lucinda. I told her I would be driving past her town so she invited us for a late lunch. Is that okay?"

"Sure, I wouldn't mind at all." Then the thought arose, a reminder of the type of people I had just left from the convention, yet here I was willing to re-engage with someone else from that community. "Umm, do you think she'll be welcoming to me?"

It probably wasn't the right question to ask your boss, especially about a member of his family, but I just wanted to be sure I was in a safe environment, I haven't been in one for the last few days.

Luca was looking ahead, but I could see that he grew confused and somewhat serious. Maybe I shouldn't have asked him that.

"Give me a moment to answer that," he finally said.

"Okay." I left it alone and stared out the window. The once-clear skies now had patches of clouds. It was still sunny, but now only partly. Luca exited the highway onto a winding road outlined with tall evergreen trees and a mansion every mile or so. We stopped at an iron gate with a hidden house deep within the trees. The gate opened, and Luca pulled into the driveway.

Lucinda's house was not the standard colonial mansion like her neighbors. It was an Italian-inspired villa, complete with a cast iron door, outdoor archways, and stone exterior. Everything about it screamed Italy.

"Oliva," Luca spoke. I turned to see cold hazel eyes pinned on me. "Regarding your question from earlier, I need you to know that I will never put you in an unsafe environment again. So, if you feel the slightest bit uncomfortable just tell me, and we'll leave. Okay?"

"Okay."

Relief settled into me. I was glad he understood, and it may have been because of what he witnessed during the convention —the disregard for me, the comments, the looks.

"Luca Bear!" A woman screamed, running out of the house. Luca stepped out to meet the thin, overly tanned, brunette woman. She took advantage of his back being turned and jumped on him. It must've been a normal thing since it didn't faze him.

"Oh my goodness." She jumped down and grabbed his cheeks. "Look how big you're getting. My little cousin is not so little anymore."

"You're only eighteen months older than me," he replied. "We were in diapers at the same time."

"Ahh, and look at us now. Grown adults. Say, where is Olivia?" She tiptoed over his shoulder and spotted me. "There you are!" She scooted Luca out of the way, reaching over to unbuckled me.

"Oh, uh, thank you." I came out to meet her.

She kissed me on my left cheek, then my right cheek, then my left again. "Sorry, I kiss on both cheeks like the French, but I always do a third kiss for good luck." She turned to Luca. "Where are your bags? The guest room is ready."

Luca shook his head. "We won't be staying the night. We'll leave shortly after lunch."

Lucinda slumped her shoulders and pouted at him. "C'mon, why not!?"

"Sorry, it wasn't in the plans today."

"All right, fine." She looped both of her arms through mine and Luca's and pulled us inside. "Let's head in. Lunch is about ready."

We walked into what I had already expected was an immaculate house, with not a speck of dust in sight. She gave us a short tour of the lower level, with all the vaulted ceilings, exposed beams, and countless unused sitting rooms. I couldn't imagine how much pressure she put on her interior designer to achieve this aesthetic.

I thought the stone kitchen was the last of the tour until she slid open the door to the backyard oasis. I could've sworn a line of drool escaped my mouth. Every plant was intentional; every tree was purposeful. It almost felt like we should've taken our shoes off before stepping onto the grass. She led us to a small banquet table in the middle of yellow lilies and blue hydrangeas.

"Luca, Olivia this my chef Don Palo. He has prepared a lovely lunch for us."

Don bowed his head then turned to Lucinda. "Would you still like to eat outside? The weather forecasts heavy rain showers."

Lucinda looked up and bit her filler-injected lips. "It's getting cloudy, but it's not raining yet. Let's enjoy the outdoors as long as we can, and if it rains, we'll head in."

"I apologize on behalf of my husband, Drew, who was supposed to join us for lunch. He's working and has locked himself in our upstairs office until further notice. Anyway, how was the conference?"

I let Luca do most of the talking as I wanted to observe his and Lucinda's relationship more closely. Lucinda was wild and free. She wouldn't let Luca finish his sentences as something would distract her and she asked him another question, then another. It didn't bother him. He laughed it off and took the frequent distraction as a time to take a sip of water. Their dynamic was cute and something I wished I had with my cousin.

"You two are pretty close," I mentioned.

Lucinda turned to me. "The closest out of all the family. It has always been 'The Adventures of Luca and Lucinda.'"

"Double L trouble," Luca chimed in.

"Yeah, well, only I would get in trouble," she corrected. "Luca is the favorite of the family. He is the epitome of a 'privileged rich boy,' and according to Aunt Deirdra, 'can do no wrong.' Could you believe that?"

"I could actually." I peered over at him.

"Speaking of Aunt Deirdra," she scooted closer to us, as she readied herself for fresh gossip. "Have you two noticed she's been acting kinda weird?"

"What do you mean?" Luca took a bite of his fettuccine and thought. "Weird, how so?"

She rolled her eyes. "Oh my goodness, never mind. Olivia, you worked with Aunt Deirdra for years now, you must know. Hasn't she seemed a little differently?"

I put down my fork and wondered what she might be alluding to. She and I know Deirdra in two different contexts:

me with work, and her with family. I was also weary of saying anything negative about someone else's family, especially to one that I just met.

Luca glanced over at me and frowned. "Lucinda, that makes her uncomfortable. Move on."

She retreated to her chair. "Excuse me, Olivia, that was not my intention at all."

But Lucinda was harmless for the most part, she wasn't like the people at the convention. "It's fine, I only work with Deirdra in a professional manner. She's been traveling to Greece quite often and seems excited about it, but that's the only difference I've seen from her this year."

Lucinda twisted her lips into a smile. "Greece, huh? That's what I've heard as well. I wonder what's in Greece."

"History, Athens, beaches, delicious food," Luca answered.

"If you say so, but don't you—oh!" Lucinda was stopped by a drop of water falling from the sky onto the table. Then another, then another. The chef rushed out to the table to grab the meal he worked hard on. "Lucinda, we have to go in now."

The four of us grabbed everything on the table in one go and hurried inside, but the rain intensified within seconds.

"*Oh cavolo!*" Don gawked at his plate of soggy fettuccine and limp bread "The food is all wet."

My bouncy curls were weighed down from the rainwater and my mascara clumped together. Having nothing to dry my face, I was about to settle for my sleeve until Luca stopped me with a napkin.

"Here, I'll help." He used his thumb to tip my chin up as he dabbed the towel across my face with gentle pressure.

My face warmed at his unexpected boldness to do it in front of his cousin, who didn't seem to care in the slightest.

"Well, looks like you two will be staying the night, it seems," she smiled deviously.

Luca continued drying my face. "The rain will pass and we'll leave after it clears up."

The rain did not pass. In fact, thunderstorms and strong winds heightened the rain's ferocity.

We were indeed staying the night.

● ● ●

After my evening shower, I changed into my silk pajamas and clipped up my hair. Lucinda gave me the corner guest room, which she'd designed in the style of a rainforest inspired retreat. It didn't match the theme of the house, but Lucinda didn't care; it's what she wanted for her guests. I figured she was the type of person to get what she wanted, regardless of whether it made sense or not, and I respected her for it.

I met her husband, Drew, during dinner. He was able to sneak away from his meeting to sit down with us. He was a typical finance guy, but much more reserved than Lucinda.

We did have something in common. Both he and I played tennis in high school and college. Tennis was his escape from the reality of his work, and his eyes brightened the more we talked about it. He even mentioned that we all should go to next year's US Open.

A subtle knock at the door caught my attention. "Come in."

Luca entered and walked up to me. He, too, had just taken a shower. His dark hair was damp, and he'd changed into his plaid pajama pants and another white T-shirt. He got to me and gave me a big whiff.

"What!" I immediately wrapped my arms around my body and stepped back.

"What soap did you use?"

"Why do you ask?"

"You don't smell like your usual sweet vanilla." He sniffed again. "More like lavender."

"Well, your cousin gave me this soap bar that she made. She said the lavender agent is supposed to help me relax."

"Yeah, she's always liked making soaps and lotions. It's always been her thing."

I put my hands on my waist and approached him. "Now that I know you sniff me, I'm curious to know—am I a lavender or vanilla girl?"

He rolled his eyes and smirked. "Oh stop, you smell me as well, and don't say that you don't. I can see your nostrils flare when I'm close."

"Well, you're always close to me!"

"Aren't you the one that just approached me with your hands at your waist? You could've asked this question from where you were."

"And may I remind you that you're the one that came into my room."

"You have a better view," he huffed.

"Of wind and rain, and apparently now lightning." I pulled back the curtain to a blurry and chaotic view of the outside. The weather had gotten worse.

He turned to me with a slanted frown. "I'm sorry about today. If we hadn't stopped for lunch we would've probably made it back home before the storm."

I shrugged. "It's all right, plus I like Lucinda and Drew. They're different than the rest. Of course I never lived the life you all did, but I felt more included today than I did during the convention."

Luca looked genuinely happy with my experience. He stayed truthful to his word and helped navigate all the conversations to make sure I felt comfortable and included.

"I'm glad," he said, and lingered around. "So, did Lucinda provide water and snacks?"

"Yep, on the nightstand."

"And you know where the remote is for the TV right?"

"Uh huh, it's on the dresser."

He looked around for anything else he'd want to mention to me. "So, do you need help with anything?"

"Nope."

"Okay, well, um goodnight, I guess. My room is down the hall if you need me."

"Goodnight Luca."

It was finally reaching midnight, but sleep had not overtaken me yet. The thunder was loud and even terrifying. Every time I closed my eyes another one struck, keeping me up. It was ridiculous; everyone else was probably fast asleep by now, and here I was struggling to close my eyes.

My mind ventured back to earlier during lunch when Lucinda teased Luca about his privileges. I thought it was harmless, but Luca seemed truly bothered by it. Even more than when I talked about it with him.

A low rumble from outside interrupted my train of thought, followed by the loudest crack I have ever heard. The lightning must've been close because the moment it happened the AC cut off. I got up to switch on the ceiling fan, but nothing happened. The power was completely out.

I felt for the doorknob and turned. The hallway was a pit of darkness, and out of curiosity I stepped out but quickly regretted it. I forgot to bring my phone as a flashlight. I looked around for anything that could help guide me, and after bumping into a few pieces of furniture, I completely lost both direction and hope.

Okay Olivia, just go to the perimeter of the hallway and feel for your doorknob.

I picked a direction and walked. When my hands finally felt drywall, I found my doorknob and entered. My foot touched the edge of the bedframe, and I bent down to plummet on the mattress.

Except I landed on a human being that happened to be my boss.

"UHHH!" he muttered out of his sleep and jolted up.

"What is this? Who is this?" He grabbed my arms.

"Ouch, Luca!" I yelped in pain.

"Olivia!" He let go of me. "Wha—what's going on. Why can't I see anything?"

"Sorry I scared you. The power is out...I came out of my room but couldn't find my way back."

"So, you tackled me?!"

"No, I thought I was in my room."

"And I thought you were an intruder. I was about to strangle you." He sighed heavily. "Are you okay?"

"I'll be fine."

His phone buzzed and he used his free hand to answer it.

"Hey... Yeah, the power is out over here too...Olivia is okay... Thanks, bye." He slid the phone back to the table but turned his phone flashlight on to give us some light. "That was Drew. The power is out on the entire street, He doesn't know when it will come back on."

"They don't have a generator?"

"Not installed yet. Worst luck."

"Hmm, okay," I yawned.

"You couldn't sleep?"

"No, the storm is too loud."

He leaned against the headboard for support, "Yeah, it's been a wicked storm."

I sighed. "When I was younger, I was always afraid of loud noises, so I never did well with thunder."

"Really? I can't see you being afraid of something like a storm."

A sudden flash of lightning lit up the room, followed by a cracking boom of thunder. It wasn't as loud as the last one, but it was long, causing me to flinch nervously.

"Whoa!" Luca pulled me back to his chest. "You *are* afraid."

"Don't tell the other managers at work. They'll never let me live it down."

He chuckled. "We all have things that we feared growing up. I don't know if we ever grew out of all of them."

I lingered on his words, then finally said, "Is there something you still fear from your past?"

"Past?" he asked. He took a while to answer, so I continued to rest my head against his soft T-shirt. I didn't think it was a tough question. He could've easily said clowns or needles, but instead he said, "Expectation."

"Expectation?" I repeated with a yawn.

"Yes," he answered in a whisper. "You okay?" He felt me shift.

"Yeah, tell me why you chose expectation."

I wish I was more alert to hear what he was saying to me, but my eyes were heavy and desperate to close.

"Olivia, are you listening?" he asked.

"Uh-huh," I yawned. "Something about your family... growing up... achieving."

"Something like that," he agreed.

And then my mind went completely blank.

8:55. I hadn't been this late to work since my tire blew two years ago. Except my tire didn't blow this morning, and I didn't wake up late. There was no reason I should be pulling up to work at 8:55. I'll have to remember that next time I want to put a little more effort into my hair and makeup.

Luca and I got back to the city early yesterday from Lucinda's house. He didn't mention anything about my intrusion from the night before, and I was glad. Honestly, I don't know how I even got back into my room after our little chat, but I'm pretty sure he carried me. It was both embarrassing and sort of cute at the same time. I parked, grabbed my lunch, laptop, coffee and ran to the entrance.

"Morning, Olivia," Trey hollered.

"Hi!" I waved.

"Let me get that door for you, Olivia." Jake rushed ahead of me to hold open the door.

"Um, thanks Jake."

Inside, the temp girls huddled in their usual corner with the Starbucks coffee in one hand and their monogrammed totes in the other. When they saw me, their eyes went from the top of my head to the bottom of my platform booties.

"Guess her clock is ticking," one of them said.

Before I could hear any more of their conversation, Sara came rushing over.

The taps of heels crashed hard against the floor with every step. Her bouncy blonde ponytail swung left to right as she walked toward me with a frown.

"Olivia!" she called out. "We need to talk!"

It was getting late, and I didn't have time to talk, so my eyes searched for an escape route.

"Oh no! You don't get out of this one." She handcuffed her arm around mine and pulled me into a corner.

"Ouch!" I pulled my arm from her. "Hey, we're going to be late."

She crossed her arm. "You didn't call me yesterday about the trip."

"Sorry, I forgot. But don't worry, I didn't forget your clothes. I'll bring them tomorrow."

She sighed. "I don't care about the damn clothes. You've been torturing me with unanswered text messages and voice-mails. I haven't had a peaceful night's rest since you left."

I couldn't help but roll my eyes at the dramatics. "Fine, I'll tell you on the way to my cubicle, but we have to keep walking."

"Yay!" She clapped happily and followed me to the elevators. I gave her the spark notes version and made sure to emphasize the strange encounters lately.

The more we talked, the happier she got.

"Oh my goodness, Olivia," she grabbed my hand. "Long car rides, room visits, outings, and you're smiling this morning."

"You're so loud."

"Don't be ridiculous!" She looked around. "No one is in this elevator; why are you even this embarrassed to talk about it—wait a second." She froze mid-sentence and stared at me hard."

"You like him."

"What! You're crazy." I moved away from her.

She moved with me. "You do! The makeup, the outfit, the smiling."

"I'm allowed to smile, Sara, and don't you want me to put more effort in the morning with my makeup and outfits anyway?" The door opened and I beelined to the breakroom, but of course Sara followed.

"Olivia, wait!" She sped up.

I opened the fridge and made room for my tuna salad behind old birthday cakes and cans of unopened Red Bull, then turned back to her.

"Don't you have work?! You missed your floor just to listen to my weekend."

"You know these are the moments I live for. Plus, everyone is dying to know, word got out that Deirdra sent you and Luca on a three-day weekend trip upstate."

"Work trip," I corrected loud enough for the nosy employees standing by the sink to hear. This was a bad place to talk, so I pulled Sara back into the hallway.

"Like I said, you two are the talk of the office," she emphasized.

I readjusted my posture and shrugged my shoulders. "It's just gossip—I'm sure it's bound to happen." My thoughts led to another trail. "Just wondering, are people talking about it on Slack?"

"Hell yeah, it's been a trending hashtag since Friday. #WhatAreTheyDoing."

My stomach dropped. "What!" I almost dropped my coffee. "You need to tell me more. What are they saying?!"

Sara raised a brow. "But it's like you said, it's all gossip and you're going to be late." She turned around and walked down the hallway, "C'mon we'll head to your department first."

"Hey, wait up, you still have to tell me!" I whispered loudly. Sara was having too much fun having the upper hand and was going to milk it for as long as she could.

"I don't think we have time, it's after nine." She laughed.

"Let's take the stairs, I'm just one more floor up."

She shivered. "Eww, no, that stairwell is creepy, and lately, people have been saying they've heard weird noises at night."

"What? Weird noses? This isn't a horror story. Plus, I'm coming with you anyway."

She obliged, and we took the hike up through the unused and poorly lit stairwell.

I tried everything to get information out of her, but she didn't budge until we got to my floor.

"Come on, tell me already."

"Listen, the hashtag didn't live past the weekend. People said you weren't the type to do anything risky anyway."

"Oh," I stepped back, offended.

"Yeah, so you've got nothing to worry about." She opened the door for me and smiled. "So, lunch in the courtyard with me and Oscar. Olivia, are you listening?"

"Huh?"

"Lunch with me and Oscar?"

"Yes, of course. See you soon."

I walked through the door but couldn't get the thought out of my head. *I wouldn't be the type to do anything.*

Sure, flirting is probably not my personality but—

"Good morning, Olivia."

"Good morning, Ashton."

—but I know how to do it and I could be—

"Good morning, Olivia."

"Good morning, Vera."

—be any type of woman I aspired to be. I dropped my things down at my desk and reached over for my cardigan and blanket, then stopped midway.

No, I will not cover my shoulders and legs today. My legs were way too accentuated in my booties, and my dress was too lovely to mask with a basic black cardigan.

"Wowza." Oscar whistled from the opening of my cubicle.

"Why is everyone making a big deal about my appearance today? Why can't I put something nice on like every other woman?"

Oscar put his hands up in surrender. "No, it's not like that at all. I just remember your first day working here and I've never seen you in something that...flattering."

I felt bad for snapping at Oscar, it wasn't his fault. "Oh okay, well just for future reference. I want you to know I can do anything any other woman can do."

Oscar burst out laughing. "So, Sara told you about the Slack hashtag, huh?"

"It's stupid." I sighed and slumped down in my chair. "Anyway, I've been dying to know... How were Thursday and Friday?"

"Two words: All. Done."

I sat up, shocked. "Really!?"

"Yep."

"Cosmetic X?"

"Completed."

"How about Harry & Dickinson?"

"The owners are pleased."

"And what about Cats&DogCo.?"

"We have them wagging their tail." He smirked. "Didn't think we could do it without you, huh? Do you have so little faith in your team?"

I smiled then rested my back against the chair.

"Thank you, Oscar. Seriously, you're the best." Oscar nodded and left to complete his duties.

But I had none of my own, at least nothing that was due yet. I sighed at the emptiness of my inbox. My mind went instantly to Luca's inbox. He probably received hundreds of emails over the course of the convention due to his position.

Where was Luca anyway? I should probably say hello, right? Especially because I haven't seen him yet. But I should also say more than that. I could ask him how his night was after the long car ride back.

Yes! That's a good idea, ask him how the night went. I stood up and took a deep breath but then stopped.

What was I doing? I needed help. Subconsciously I opened the phone to text Sara for ideas, then stopped again.

Did I really not know how to casually engage in a conversation with a man, preferably about something that didn't have to do with work?

I put down my phone and began walking to his office. It didn't matter what I did or didn't have experience with. I'm good at trying new things and will excel when given the opportunity.

Or maybe not. The chair was empty. His premium leather backpack was nowhere to be found, solidifying his absence. He wasn't here.

My mood deflated faster than a balloon that had just popped. I sighed so loudly my employees could probably hear me outside, but I didn't care. A flood of emotions ran through me. None of which I was able to pinpoint as to why.

"Olivia."

His voice.

I gasped. "Luca?"

He stood closer than where I expected him to be. He was in an all-black outfit of slacks and matching polo. His freshly washed hair swayed to one side. The opposing but attractive smells of cedar and clean laundry were adamant in his proximity, so much so that I had to stop myself from stepping closer.

He tilted his head and stared intently at me. "Were you looking for me?"

"Sort of." It was the only answer I could think of since there was no work-related reason I'd be in his office.

He broke eye contact to put his bag down and open his laptop. "So, you just randomly stand in people's offices, sort of looking for them."

It sounded ridiculous when he put it like that, but I already said it, so I had to own it.

"Yes, I do."

"Well then, I was sort of looking for you too, but you weren't in your cubicle."

My heart froze. "Wait, really, why? Did you need something? Am I in trouble?"

Luca laughed. "No, Olivia. I just wanted to see you, that's all. It had nothing to do with work."

"Oh." My eyes briefly drifted away from him but soon returned as there was nothing else interesting in the office to look at.

"You still don't like my office," he glanced up from his laptop.

"I never said that."

"You said it with your eyes." He waited. "Good thing you're getting better at lying."

I walked around and thought. "You should decorate, put diplomas up. Order some trinkets for your desk, and a family picture maybe? I guarantee more people will visit you."

"People do visit my office. Managers, employees, everyone comes," he corrected. He walked to the front of the desk and leaned against it. Hazel eyes searched mine. "Now that I think about it, you're the only one who doesn't visit me except for the first day that I moved in and today, which you still haven't told me the real reason as to why."

"I did," I argued.

"I asked if you were looking for me. You said, 'sort of.' He continued his prying attitude, this time with a cocky grin. "Olivia, why are you in my office?"

He asked it the same way a parent would ask their child, slow and clear. Why was he so stuck on the 'why?' It reminded me of my father when he was trying to teach me something.

"What are you trying to get at?" I finally asked. I wasn't in the mood to play this game with him.

"Directness," he simply answered. "But I think I'm getting closer, so I'll drop it."

"What a waste of time," I mumbled underneath my breath and headed for the door.

"Olivia, wait."

I stopped.

"Are you available this afternoon at five? I need assistance to navigate the manager's master file?"

"The Managerial Master File? And you want *me* to teach *you*?"

"Yes." He nodded confidently.

I stood tall and proud, happy that I had finally had the upper hand. "Then I must let you know I'm a tough teacher."

"And I'm a quick learner."

"I will make you cry."

"I'll bring a box of tissues."

"We'll definitely be here past working hours."

"I'll order us dinner."

Of course, he had an answer for everything. My first time working with the master file took me months to get right. It was something Deirdra takes quite seriously.

"Okay, but navigating the master file is a pivotal task in the director's position, so I will be noting it in my journal."

"I hope you do. See you at five, Olivia."

• • •

The sound of laptops closing and office chairs being pushed in wasn't new to me. Employees made it a point to leave promptly, especially on Mondays. After accepting the manager role, I came to terms with the fact that I'd rarely ever leave on time to see the sun set again.

Oscar knocked on my cubicle wall. "Hey, just wanted to say bye for the day. Sorry I can't stay tonight. I'm meeting Maria for bowling."

"Maria, the same Maria from over a month ago?"

He blushed immediately. "Yeah, it's going well. Almost too well. I'm telling you Olivia, falling in love is like a dream that I never want to wake up from."

I couldn't remember seeing Oscar this happy in a very long time. After his last breakup, he took some time off from dating and was unsure if he ever wanted to try again. Oscar, in his own way, was like Sara, except Sara found her soulmate, so I could only hope that Oscar was getting closer to his.

"Also, thanks for leading Team B while Cecile is off. I know that you don't have to, but it'll relieve some of her stress when she comes back from maternity leave."

"That's what I'm here for." Oscar waved goodbye then left through the back door.

My alarm clock buzzed.

"5:00: Train Luca on Master File," it read.

I gathered my things and got up, only to be stopped by Luca standing at my cubicle with an extra office chair and laptop.

"Oh, were you coming to me?"

Luca proceeded to enter. "Yes, after your comment this morning, I deemed my office not suitable for your presence."

He did his best to hide his grin from me but couldn't last five seconds without looking in my direction.

His whole act made me snort, which in turn made me cover my nose in embarrassment.

He stopped. "You're a snorter?!"

"No!" Heat rushed to my face. "I mean—I've never snorted before."

This was getting ridiculous. "Never mind, just come in." I scooted my chair and laptop to make room for him.

It took a while to start. Luca had to take a call with an upset manager, Chrissy. A few employees stopped by to ask questions about upcoming projects. Most blinked twice when they saw Luca sitting comfortably next to me on his phone. I could only imagine what Slack would look like tonight.

Chrissy had Luca on the phone for thirty minutes. It took every ounce of restraint not to ask what she was crying about now, since every Monday she was crying about something ridiculous.

"Uh huh, thanks, Chrissy." Luca brought his call to an end and put down his phone with a heavy sigh of exhaustion.

"Are you all mine now? Because I really don't want to share you with Chrissy," I teased.

It meant to be lighthearted, but Luca kept a straight face. "I need to be accessible to all managers, you know that."

"Of course." I turned away immediately. "I know that."

"But," he went on, "I will always come back to you afterward."

Everything about what he said was professional, but it made my heart flutter, and I instantly lost track of what I was doing.

"You know, she's looking to retire next year. We're going to need to find a new marketing manager." He paused. "What do you think about Liam Frasier?"

"As a replacement manager? I'd say yes, but I am biased because I interviewed him when Chrissy was on vacation."

Luca moved to the edge of the seat. "What did you like about him?"

"His dedication," I say. "Data driven, Strategic thinker, creative, adaptable. He'll go an extra one hundred miles for a client, but only if he deems it worth it." I frowned. "Part of this business is having faith in our clients and their dreams. Once he gets there, I will be sure he'll be a phenomenal manager."

"Something to think about." Luca nodded.

We took a moment to enjoy the quietness of the empty office, just the two of us. It was an ongoing joke that the managers can only get work done when everyone leaves for the day, but there was so much truth to it.

Luca hung on his suit jacket behind his chair, and loosen up his shirt buttons. He ran his fingers through his hair and gave it a good ruffle until it pointed every direction.

"Am I not worthy to impress?" I asked. "Now that everyone's gone, there's no need for Luca Lontern to put any effort anymore, huh?"

Luca stared at me in shock.

I spun around to him and crossed my legs with exaggeration. "Oh, and you're speechless. That's a win for me."

"I just never thought you saw me in such a light, that's all." He smiled as he received the upper hand.

"Whatever, just open your laptop so we can start."

The first half of our time was spent teaching just the foundation of the Master File, and why we use it, but Luca was quite distracted. His eyes kept drifting from the computer screen, then to me, then to the pictures pinned on my walls.

Ding. His phone's obnoxious ringer interrupted my teaching.

"That's the third time. Do I need to confiscate your phone?" I warned.

"It's our dinner, Olivia. Remember, I promised to feed you in exchange for your time."

"One meal for two hours of my evening might not equate, Mr. Lontern."

"Then I'll have to make it up to you some more." He left before I could offer a rebuttal.

Minutes flew by and he still hadn't returned, so I peeked over at his notepad. One hour of teaching and he had two things written: his name and date, which were accompanied by the BSG letterhead.

My mood dropped as a thought arose: maybe I was a boring teacher, and he wasn't retaining any of the information.

I reached for my phone to ask Google "creative ways to teach adults" when a noise behind me caught my attention.

"Hello?" I swung around.

Except no one was there, just the door to the stairwell. I went back to my phone when the sounds began again. My mind remembered back to when Sara mentioned earlier about the creepy stairwell sounds.

The footsteps returned.

"Luca?"

No answer. My heart sped up as Sara's theory started to sound less crazy.

This is ridiculous, I've stayed late many times and never heard such a noise. I walked over to the door and leaned my head against it, listening closely to what may or may not be on the other side.

Quiet, just as I thought. I pushed open the door to confirm my conclusion.

A six-foot man stood across from me. Black hair, gray shirt, sunken face, large eyes. Not Luca, not security, not anyone I've seen here before.

"Eeek!" I dropped my phone and ran in the opposite direction, straight to the elevators. I abused the elevator button like a kid in an arcade.

"C'mon, c'mon, c'mon." It took a second or two, but the second elevator opened. I rushed in, then hit the button for the lobby.

Thankfully, the middle elevator was the fastest and arrived in the lobby in less than a minute.

The door opened and I sprinted out. Luca was only mere yards away from me.

From afar he held up a brown bag in his hand, and yelled, "Sorry for the wait, I was talking to the delivery ma—"

I didn't care about dinner or why it was late. I just needed to be away from the trespasser on the eighth floor.

There was only two feet of distance between Luca and I before I leaped off the floor and crashed into him. Luca's eyes widened as he immediately dropped the brown bag to safely catch me. Firm hands caught me by my waist. My arms wrapped around his neck and locked themselves there.

"Whoa, Olivia," he blurted.

I dug my head safely in the cover of his armpit.

"Olivia?" He asked once he noticed that I couldn't stop shaking.

"There's someone upstairs," I mumbled into his shirt.

"What? Olivia, I can't hear you."

I lifted my head and looked up at him, resting my chin on his chest.

"I said there's someone upstairs. I have never seen this person before." I closed my eyes to try and remember what he looked like. "He is tall, and uh... skinny, and his face is sunken, and—"

My voice couldn't go on without trembling. My body hadn't relaxed yet.

"Okay. Okay," he whispered to me. "I'm right here, Olivia. No one is going to hurt you."

I closed my eyes and took deep, slow breaths. Luca wrapped his arms tighter around me for reassurance.

It took a few moments, but my grip around his neck loosened, and I was able to relax.

He felt it and smiled sweetly at me, but that changed once he started asking serious questions.

"Are you sure you've never seen this person before?"

"Certain."

"Did he hurt you?"

"No, I ran from him. I didn't look back to see if he was running after me, I mean maybe he was, but I'm not sure."

Luca thought, his eyes moved left to right as he was trying to find an answer, then released me. "I'm going to check."

I pulled him back. "What no! We have to call the police and notify Deirdra and—"

"You don't trust that I can't handle it?" he asked abruptly.

"No, that's not it. You're clearly well built." My hand slid down his biceps. "And I know you'd defend yourself, but what if he has a knife or gun?"

He laughed, but that irritated me more, I was far from joking.

I crossed my arms and blocked him from the elevator. "I am serious, he could be dangerous."

Luca dropped his attitude to match mine. "Listen, you can contact the police, but let me at least check it out first. It might be all a misunderstanding."

I blew a sharp breath. He was downplaying everything?!

"Fine, I'm going with you then."

"Absolutely not," he answered firmly. "Stay here."

I stepped back, surprised. He was serious—more serious than I was. Luca never had to yell to get his point across. He just needed to use his voice, in a particular tone to be taken seriously, but it still wasn't fair.

"So, *you're* allowed to check it out, because 'it might be a misunderstanding,' but if I come along for that same reason, then it's 'absolutely not'?"

He knew I got him there, but that didn't stop him from winning. "Listen, I'll check it out first, then you can come."

"Fine, you've got three minutes."

He left in the elevator, and I couldn't help but stand there idly watching the numbers climb to floor number eight. Maybe I should've called the police, but I just stood there with our takeout food in hand trying not to spiral about what may or may not be happening.

If something was happening, I couldn't hear it—I was several floors down. My hand clenched into a tight fist. Why did I listen to Luca? Three minutes passed and he still hadn't come back.

After what seemed like forever, the elevator descended. I braced myself for who might appear.

The door opened, and Luca stood proudly next to the unknown man.

"Olivia, this is Eric, the new nightly custodian."

Eric passed me my phone, "Sorry, miss, I didn't mean to scare you earlier."

"I should be apologizing. It was an overreaction on my part."

"We'll make sure to provide you with a name badge moving forward," Luca cut in. "Again, sorry to interrupt your duties."

Eric nodded and left, while Luca and I took the elevator back upstairs in silence.

"I feel like a complete idiot," I admitted after returning to my desk.

Luca opened our Thai takeout. "Don't worry about it. I'll mention Eric's new employment in this week's memo."

I didn't want to admit to him that no one read the company's memos, but maybe it was just to avoid future incidents.

He took out an assortment of small dishes, all of which we were supposed to pick from.

I started on the edamame first. "I didn't know you like Thai food."

"Yeah, me and my buddies toured in Asia a few summers back, and we spent a good amount of time in Thailand. Don't get me wrong, Thai Kitchen is good, but it doesn't compare to what I tasted in Thailand."

"Most of my summers were spent catering on the side to pay off student loans, but you know, experiencing the cultural diversity of Asia would've been nice too." I smirked at him, the same smirking he does to me when he wants my reaction to something.

His expression faded. "Sorry I didn't mean to gloat, I just thought I'd mention why I like Thai food."

Usually, I'd agree that he was flashing his comfy life in my face, but that wasn't Luca—at least not what I've seen of him thus far. I decided to take it a step further.

"Oh, well, I was." I shrugged. "You missed out on holding an eight-glass champagne tray at a spoiled twenty-two-year-old's bridal shower. "

He snickered, "Yeah well attending those spoiled twenty-two-year-old weddings is no easy feat either. Having to encounter superficial lifestyles should be a sport."

We couldn't help but continue to one up each other on who had it worse; having to travel every summer versus staying home for two months straight, private school drama versus public school craziness.

The debate continued for another hour and well into our

walk back to my car. Luca was invested in my stories of the working-class life while I much rather preferred to get his take on his recent travels to South Africa.

We stopped in our tracks. The car was several feet away, though I wished it was further. It was the point where we'd say goodnight and drive home in opposite directions, but neither of us were ready to initiate it.

A cool fall breeze sung softly into the night. We stood across from each other in complete silence. Even in the dark of night, Luca's hazel eyes glowed brightly.

But it wasn't just his eyes that I was captivated with—it was his messy hair, his arrogant nose, his slim lips. It was his masculine physique and excessive height. He was different from me in every way. Growing up, I never would have been caught with someone so opposite in lifestyle, looks, and upbringing, and yet here I was not wanting to part ways.

How did I arrive here?

"Luca," I uttered.

The second his name rolled off my lips, he stepped forward, shortening the distance between us. His eyes searched mine intently, invading any privacy that I reserved for myself. It was as if he was trying to find something in me, so he rummaged freely through my thoughts, until he stopped. His eyes slowly but carefully dropped their focus from my gaze to my nose, to my lips, which he lingered on before traveling back up to my eyes. And just like that, he began to lean in.

My heart, which for the entirety of my life beat to the pace of a ticking clock increased to the speed of a hummingbird. Like any second-place runner trying to win gold, my breathing struggled to catch up.

I stumbled back in response, but restriction followed when my body hit against the cold metal door of my Jeep.

"Are you okay?" Luca asked as he continued his pursuit.

"Yes, umm, I think I am." Having nowhere to run, my hands rested against my car. Why? I don't know. My entire vision was of his face. The air from his nose is felt against my lips.

"We should go," I say. "It's late."

"I know," he whispers back.

"There's tons of meetings tomorrow."

"As there always is." He drops his eyelids halfway.

His nose finally meets mine, and caresses it like a lion to his lioness. My eyes close and I savor the moment.

"And you can't be late you are...you are..." I can't finish my thought. My mind is mush and I can't form the words.

"I am what? Tell me."

"The boss," my voice mutters.

Like a director, saying a cut. Our moment takes an abrupt stop. He sighs, and he steps away.

Bright lights in the distance shone on us. Both Luca and I turned to see Vince, our nighttime security guard, driving his car.

"Aye," he yelled. "Are you two good?"

Luca shot him a thumbs up.

Vince nodded and scratched his head. "Sorry to interrupt."

Luca brushed it off. "All good Vince, do you mind driving me to my car. It's a bit of a hike from where I am."

Vince agreed, and Luca opened my car door hinting to get in. There was no way of resuming the night.

I stepped in. "Goodnight, Luca."

"Goodnight, Olivia." He closed the door and walked off to join Vince in his car. I watched the taillights disappear around the back end of the building.

It wasn't until I turned on my car that I realized the one thing I never thought could cross my mind: I wanted to kiss the very person who stole my job, my boss, Luca Lontern.

He had taken residency in my work life, and now he was reserving space in my personal life as well.

9

Three a.m., and after tossing and turning, I couldn't find a decent sleeping position that was suitable to doze off. My cat watched me wrestle with myself from the corner of my bed. I got up too many times for a sip of water, bathroom runs, and late-night snacks.

Olivia, just close your eyes and relax.

But after a minute my eyes were wide open. I ripped my floral comforter off my body and switched on my ceiling fan. My room was like an oven, and I needed some cool air.

I laid back on my pillow and knew that it was neither the heat, nor hunger, nor an overactive bladder that was keeping me up. It was Luca.

Ugh. I covered my face with my pillow. "Why is this happening to me?"

Luca was my boss. It's not illegal to want this; heck, most women wanted a kissing session with Luca, I shouldn't feel weird. It's only natural.

I let go of the pillow and listened to it drop onto the floor. Memories of this past weekend arose, making me wish it never ended. It was better than I expected. With Luca I felt at home like I was meant to be there because he wanted me there, specifically beside him during the cocktail hour, during breakfast, and everywhere else.

My favorite was the bar, where his fingers couldn't stop caressing my arm. Sure, I got a sly remark from our waitress and stares from surrounding guests. It was something I'd grown accustomed to whenever I'm around him.

I wish we could continue our conversation from earlier. We called it a night too soon, and could've gone longer, way longer.

My eyes gradually closed as I thought it over, and soon after drifting off, the traumatizing beep of my alarm sounded.

"Oh," I moaned and checked the alarm. There was no time to hit the snooze button. My new makeup routine took up any spare minutes I allowed myself.

The shower was a good wake-up call. I poured myself a bowl of Special K and pondered on a way to get myself out of this predicament.

The more time I spent with him, the worse my infatuation became. So, on my morning commute, I decided—no more Luca. Of course, I couldn't avoid him completely; he was my boss, and we would cross paths eventually. But I could draw a line. Work only. No after-hours. No trips.

This was the only way to silence the romantic thoughts about him.

● ● ●

I scrolled through the last slide of Lexi's presentation to our client, Wash & Go Car. It wasn't for any Business Class clients, not even our Midgrade clients, but for our In Town clients, which she still wasn't happy with.

After two years of employment, Lexi maintained a healthy list of Midgrade clientele, so assigning her an In Town client was considered "newbie status" and "moving backwards", as she has stated in her email to me. She did, in fact, attach the presentation to the email, so at least she got over it.

"Thanks for the presentation, I'll send you my evaluation by the end of the week- Olivia" and send!

"She's still going to be upset. She was talking about you in the break room this morning," Oscar said from behind.

"You know, one day you won't be able to spy on my emails. I'll put up a privacy screen."

"If you wanted to put a privacy screen on, you would've done it by now." He paused. "Wait, why is that here?" he referred to the spare chair in the corner.

"It's Luca's."

"Oh?" His voice heightened. "Well, you must've had a great time last night considering he's not here."

"He is not here?" I held my breath.

"Well not yet, at least," he corrected me. "Sorry, didn't mean to give you a heart attack."

"Oh stop, you didn't give me a heart attack." I spun back to my computer. "I just had a couple of budgets that I needed him to approve, but I'll just wait until later."

"Definitely a heart attack," he mumbled under his breath.

I was about to give him a full-fledged rebuttal when a message came in from Deirdra.

Deirdra: "Hey, can you meet me in my office? It'll be quick. Bring a notepad and pen."

"Duty calls." I stood up and gathered my things. Oscar smirked. He knew he got the last word.

"Can you check in on Lexi and smooth things over for me?" I pouted.

"Sure, Your Majesty," he bowed.

"Thanks, and it wasn't a heart attack." I rushed out before he could say anything else. I made sure to pass Luca's office before heading to the elevators. Empty. Well, it wasn't exactly empty, it had everything an office should have: a desk, cabinet, bookshelf, everything but a human.

When I reached Deirdra's office, I gently tapped on the door and waited for her usual "yes," which in her terms meant "come in."

I tapped again but heard no answer. Was she in today? She had to be; she just messaged me to meet her in her office.

"Hey." I looked over at Abby, who had been scrolling on social media since I arrived. "Is Deirdra here today?"

"Huh, what?" Abby stopped twirling her fingers around her hair and put down her phone.

"Is. Deirdra. Here. Today?" I repeated.

"Uh, yeah, yeah." She walked to the door then proceeded to open it.

With her legs crossed on her desk, Deirdra leaned back on her chair, smiling from ear to ear as she stared at her phone. She hadn't even realized we walked in.

"Ms. Deirdra," Abby called.

"Oh!" She dropped her relaxed pose and repositioned herself in a more professional manner. "Sorry, dear."

Abby left us alone and returned to desk.

Deirdra smiled at me, but it was so strange to see her in an enjoyable mood. The rumors were true.

"Thanks for coming." She grinned.

"What did you want to talk about?"

"Talk about? Oh—yes." She snapped out of it and went on. "I don't know if you noticed, but Luca isn't here today."

"I noticed."

"Yes, my dear nephew is sick today, poor thing. He wanted to come in, but I insisted that he stay home and get better."

"Smart call," I said flatly.

Deirdra peered at me, clearly desperate to know what my

deal was this morning. I wanted to unleash all the resentment I had for her, but it wasn't time yet. I hadn't quite saved up six months of emergency funds in case I got fired.

"And since you're the most qualified manager, I informed him that you would take care of his workload while he's out."

This was the most unnerving thing about Deirdra. She assigns me tasks before asking me, then justifies it by saying I'm the most qualified. The only good part was that she admitted that I was equally as qualified as Luca.

I begrudgingly opened my notepad. "What needs to be done?

We went through the to-do list, and I headed downstairs to get started. Thankfully, the work was nothing new to me. Our former director, Chris, was absent religiously, so Deirdra frequently asked me to be acting director.

While I hated the way she communicated my new tasks, it was the baptism by fire that made me qualified for higher positions.

I sighed, and sent my last task in at 5:04 p.m., making sure to cc Luca and Deirdra on everything I did. Today dragged on, and I wasn't sure why. Usually when I cover another manager's work, especially the director's, time flies by.

"Olivia!" Sara cried then hugged me from behind. "I missed you." She let go and hopped on my desk, letting her foot dangle off the edge.

"Hey," I moaned. "Today was so long."

She cracked up. "That's my line! You love work."

"I know, so I don't know why today dragged on." I yawned. "Maybe because I didn't get much sleep last night."

Sara grabbed my bag and began packing my things.

"Wait, what are you doing?" I got up to stop her.

"No!" She swung my bag away from me. "There's a happy

hour, everyone is going, including us. You've been looking too good lately, and we can't let your beauty go to waste. C'mon."

I had no energy to stop her, so I went along with her plan. Sara spent the drive updating me on the newest hire at BSG— William from Finance, otherwise known as her newest prospect for me. Strangely, Oscar hadn't told her about my evening with Luca yesterday, and I was glad. After the emotional roller coaster I'd been having about him, I didn't need Sara to influence me on the Luca topic anymore.

We arrived and the bar was packed wall-to-wall with BSG employees. I was even shocked to see some managers present.

"Whoa, whoa!" A man shouted from the corner. It was Connor, Sara's manager from Sales. "Do my eyes deceive me? Is that Olivia?!"

Connor was loud, entitled, and always had an entourage around him. He, alone, was the reason why HR updated the training quarterly.

I remember my first time meeting Connor. We'd been assigned a joint project by Deirdra, long before we'd been promoted to managers, and like most encounters I've had at BSG, we were polar opposites.

The first thing he ever said to me once we sat down was that he had a Black friend back in fourth grade. I didn't know what to make of such a greeting, other than that he was trying to find some common ground between us. It was an unnecessary statement, but seeing that it was harmless, I just smiled and opened my laptop. It wasn't the response he'd hoped for, so he added that he'd never dated a Black girl before, and was hopeful for what the future might hold.

It was in that moment I realized I would never consider any man from BSG a viable prospect.

"I didn't think Ms. Workaholic would show up. Here, you

need some alcohol." He grabbed a beer from a passing waiter and handed it to me.

"Connor!" I nudged him. "You just stole someone's beer!"

"It's yours now." He shrugged, then turned around and shouted. "Aye, cheers to Olivia!"

I didn't see them before, but Rasheed, Janet, Brad, Brenda— oh, the entire management team was here. They played it smart, keeping their distance from the employees. Half of them laughed uncontrollably; the rest made jokes that would've justified a write-up. I did my best to integrate, but in hindsight, I'd never willingly spend free time with these people outside of work.

"So, did you get your raise yet?" Brenda questioned. She was staring at me from the corner.

"Excuse me?"

"You know, since you're always with Luca? All that hard work should pay off somehow, right?"

"If I get a raise, it's because I work hard and I show results," I clarified. "So, if you want a raise, then work hard. Simple."

She stepped back, insulted. "Hey, you don't need to get defensive. I am all for women empowerment. Listen, us women need to climb the corporate ladder by whatever means possible. All I am saying is I wouldn't judge how someone gets there."

"Hey, ladies, why the tension?" Connor draped his arms around us. His breath reeked of alcohol. "Brenda, is this about Olivia going to the convention again? Listen, Brendy, can I call you that? Great. So, you have to let it go. Olivia got to go with the most wanted man in all of BSG, and not you. Heck, we all wanted her spot." He laughed. "But it's not our story."

"Whatever, Connor." She pushed his arm away from her. "You were saying the same thing before she came in."

He didn't flinch even though she'd ratted him out. Instead, he gulped down his beer and slammed it on the table.

"Olivia, listen." He bent down, and he lowered his voice. "Whatever happened at the convention, stays at the convention, and don't let anyone tell you otherwise," he said with a slur.

That was my cue to find Sara and leave. If I stayed any longer with the drunk manager crew, someone would get murdered.

I spotted her blonde ponytail first. She sat at the bar with Oscar and another gentleman.

"Did you have fun with your colleagues?" Sara asked with a smile.

"It depends on your definition of fun. Anyway, I came back to say goodbye."

"What! It's only been fifteen minutes."

"It's been an hour." I showed her my watch.

"Okay, but first, meet William." She leaned back on the chair so I could get a good look at him.

William was already looking at me. Sara was right, he was cute, his face was a kind reminder of an early 2000's Channing Tatum, but a lot tanner. He managed a smile, then held out his hand.

"Oliva, right? It's nice to finally meet you."

I shook his warm hand. "Finally?" I asked.

He scratched his head and thought. "Yes, well I've heard a lot about you since I started working here last week. You're famous at BSG."

"Well, apparently not to everyone." I looked back at the manager table.

William frowned, seeing that the comment bothered me. He might've regretted even mentioning it, but it didn't matter. BSG gossip has followed me since the first day working with the company.

"Let's see... Something about, 'Olivia is the go-to person here,' 'Olivia trained me,' 'I can always count on Olivia,'" he said with a grin.

I laughed, knowing some were exaggerated truths, but I appreciated his effort to make me smile. The waiter came back with two spritzes. It wasn't what I ordered. In fact, I don't think I ordered anything. They must've been for Oscar and Sara, but they had left to another table and were too deep in other conversations to come back.

"Well, it would be rude to waste an unclaimed, paid for drink, wouldn't you say?" William winked. He took the two glasses off the tray and slid one over to me. "So, Olivia, who should we make this toast to?"

I stared at the small bubbles racing to the top of the glass and thought about my answer. "Let's make this toast to us and to all the hangovers that everyone will endure tomorrow. Cheers."

William wasn't as bad as I thought. He graduated from the same university I'd attended but two years later. We probably even passed each other on campus once or twice. He lived ten minutes from me at a sister apartment complex. I gave him advice on how to deal with his manager, Jason, and pointers on how to better transition into his position. His good company was an interesting turn of events to a busy day, so much so that I left the restaurant knowing, outside of Sara and Oscar, I might've made a new friend. It was just the distraction I needed from Luca.

10

I t was a bun type of hair day, tightly slicked back with two scoops of gel. When I finally was able to get my hair to the desired glossed look, I carefully slipped my black dress over my head and zipped up. My car ride, which was usually me rambling to myself, was reduced to a podcast on the various benefits of learning how to juggle.

I stopped at the light and glanced at the dashboard. My check engine light lit back up. It was an on-and-off thing since last year. I promised myself that I'd bring my car to the mechanic if the light stayed on for at least seven days straight. The longest it had lasted was four.

I arrived at my usual parking space but at eight fifty-eight and rushed out of the car and into the building.

"Mornin', Dale!" I shouted over my shoulder. Guilt rushed over me when I heard him say "good morning" back, but there was no time to chat. I squeezed into the elevator just before the door shut.

"Look who made it in the nick of time." I turned to see Connor pressed against the wall with his laptop in one hand, coffee in another, and sunglasses sitting on his nose.

The oversized aviators were his attempt to hide a massive hangover, but to me they only highlighted how stupid he was last night.

"You're going to have to take off your sunglasses eventually," I whispered to him. "People are going to think you're weird for wearing sunglasses inside."

"Shh," he whispered. "I have a massive hangover."

"Oh, who would've thought." I shook my head in surprise.

"Yeah, thankfully Luca is out again, so we're in the clear."

I gulped. "Luca is out again?"

"Yeah, Shane just texted me. Anyway, I think I'll hide under my desk until lunch time. The hangover should pass by then."

"Oh."

"Yeah, don't look so sad. This is like a free day for managers," he said before exiting out to his floor.

"I am not sad!" But it was too late, and the elevator had already shut.

Connor knew very little about me. I wasn't sad. Stress, yes, but not sad. For yet again, I would have to take on Luca's work-load. Connor didn't have to do that, so how would he know how I felt?

I walked past Luca's dark office and sighed. "Another long day."

• • •

Bing! With my hands still hovering over the keyboard, I peeked over at my phone.

One New Message from William. Usually, I didn't like checking my phone while I was in the midst of responding to angry clients, but my mind was a mess at this point and I needed a break from it all. I clicked open.

William: Hey! Are you alive?

Me: After two cups of coffee I am.

William: It takes me at least three to four.

Me: That would have me working from the restroom all day. LOL

William: It's a good detox. Btw, I wanted to thank you for giving me pointers about Jason.

I "Liked" the message and put down my phone. It was time to get back to work. Just as I got ready to write another round of appeasement emails, William texted back.

William: Do you want to grab lunch during break?

I couldn't help but smile, and I knew exactly why. It's been years since I've been asked out by the opposite sex with no work attached to it, just a get to know you sort of thing.

Me: Yeah, let's go.

William forewarned me about possibly running late, so I used the time to clean out my bag, an overdue chore that is best done when given spare minutes.

Old lip gloss—toss.

Empty package of gum—toss.

Crumpled receipt—toss.

I paused after the receipt and looked at the half-filled trash can. My father always told me to hold receipts for as long as you can, even if it was a purchase of mints.

"You never know if you need it," he'd say.

It was wise advice, but it also contributed to his hoarding problem. I picked up the crumpled paper, after deciding that I should at least read it.

It was a Taco Bell receipt from our road trip last weekend; two nachos, two medium sodas, one bean burrito, and one chicken enchilada. Originally, he wanted the bean burrito, but I insisted the chicken enchilada was better. He didn't believe me until he saw cheese oozing out of mine. I cut him an untouched half, and we traded.

"Hey, you ready?"

"Oh!" I flinched, unaware of William's sudden presence behind me. "I didn't see you there." I tossed the receipt back at the desk and threw on my wool coat. "Yeah, let's go."

We decided on a local cafe, a short walk from the office. Inside, we found the perfect table tucked into a corner while we awaited our food.

This cafe was quite popular with staff who didn't want to go too far for lunch, but were also tired of BSG cafeteria food.

"Do you watch thrillers?" William asked after coming back with our sodas.

"Hmm?" I had to think. I didn't want to tell him that work consumed all aspects of my life and I couldn't even remember the last time I enjoyed a Netflix series, but it was the truth.

"I haven't watched thrillers in a while. You'll need to send me a list so I can start something this weekend. Promise?" I held up my pinky to him.

He tilted his head perplexed at my childlike version of a promise, so I had to double down on it.

"Don't look at me like that!" I teased. "This is the best type of a contract nowadays and you know it."

He wrapped his large pinky around mine, his eyes squinting with humor. "Bet, I'll start making you a list tonight."

A waiter with a large tray stopped by, placing a grilled cheese sandwich with tomato soup in front of William and a tuna sandwich with broccoli cheddar soup in front of me.

Lunch with William wasn't awkward at all. We kept bouncing between our favorite sci-fi stories: mine was *Star Wars*, while he swore *Star Trek* was better. From that point we moved on to our favorite music genres. Surprisingly, we both liked alternative rock. That's when he admitted to me that he never went to a Paramore concert. I told him never to talk to me again about music until he goes to one. William laughed uncontrollably, which in turn stole the attention of everyone in the dining room. He had a signature laugh, the type that sounded like how it was spelled, but it was so genuine and contagious it made me laugh as well.

Halfway into our meal, William's eyes drifted down at my plate. I'd barely touched my sandwich. "You know, you should try dipping your sandwich in your soup. It'll taste better."

My stomach turned at the sound of his suggestion. "Eww, that only works with tomato soup and grilled cheese."

He wasn't buying it, so I tore him off a piece of my sandwich and let him dip it into the soup.

He was so confident in his hypothesis that he took a large bite and chewed. I observed his eyes widening the longer he tumbled it in his mouth.

Within seconds he scurried for a napkin, covered his mouth and it spit out.

"Sorry you had to witness that." He crumpled the napkin into a ball.

I leaned back in victory, "If only you'd listened, Luca. I would've saved your taste buds."

Luca?!

"I am so sorry." I resumed my position and scratched my head. "I don't know where that came from."

William sipped his soda and shrugged. "It's all right, you've called me that three times already."

"Have I?" Heat consumed my face.

"Yep, does he scare you or something? I haven't met him yet, but the fact that you keep calling me Luca makes me wonder."

"No," I said a little too quickly. "I mean, I have to cc him on everything and there are some joint projects we're working on." That was more information than he'd asked for. I'm starting to sound like Sara. "Anyway, Luca isn't scary at all. I just have a lot of things at work to get done. That's all."

We got back to work a few minutes late. I told William if Jason is still giving him problems to come and speak to me and I would settle it for him. It was the little power I'd been granted—manager privilege—and I used it sparingly. But William was still new, and I didn't want him to get into the slightest bit of trouble.

People were definitely more relaxed knowing that Luca wasn't at the gate to greet them. He usually stands bravely among the incoming crowds. I slowed down to watch the same crowds of people stroll in with no care of time. As busy as it was in the lobby, without him it felt so empty.

Things were back to normal by the time I got to my floor. Cubicles were filled and calls were being made. I came back to a brown bag sitting on my desk.

"What's this?" I asked, knowing Oscar would answer.

"Uber Eats came about ten minutes ago." Oscar called out.

I didn't call for takeout. I unclipped the bag to find a steamy enchilada from Taco Bell hidden inside.

My hand searched my bag for my phone, hoping it was give me a clue.

One New Message from Job Stealer:

Job Stealer: Thank you for taking care of things while I am out. Enjoy your lunch and take a big bite for me.

I sat down to take a bite of its cheesy goodness, closing my eyes in utter delight. Did I just eat? Yes. Should I eat another meal? Maybe not, but for some reason that I wasn't ready to admit out loud, I've been craving Taco Bell all day.

• • •

Luca's absentees didn't stop there. They continued on the next day and the next and even on Friday.

I closed my laptop and breathed a sigh of relief. It was two p.m. on Friday, and somehow, I got everything done—mine and Luca's.

Just as I was about to lay back on my chair a voice shot me straight up. It wasn't the sound that scared me, but who it was coming from.

"Oliva, dear."

"Deirdra?" I stood up and turned around to see her in an all-white linen dress and a messy blond bun staring at me.

"Yes, are you surprised?"

"Well, I never thought you would come down to my desk. I usually come up to your office."

She crossed her arms and looked away shyly. "Well, it's never too late to turn a new leaf. I believe that's how the saying goes."

"Yes, but for you—" I began to say, "actually, never mind. Were we supposed to meet? Because I didn't receive any invite."

"No, I just want to thank you for all the hard work you put in this week with my nephew being out."

"Uh huh," I nodded. This surely wasn't the only reason she walked down from her throne all the way to us peasants. "And?"

"And I wanted to ask you one more favor."

"What is it?" I took out my notepad, ready to jot down her laundry list of to-dos.

"It's not anything work related." She scooted behind me to sit in my office chair.

Oh okay, this is what we're doing now. I leaned against my filing cabinet and acted as if the corners weren't impaling my butt cheeks.

"So, what's up?"

"My dear Luca has been sick these past few days. Poor thing has been running a fever, and I don't know what he's been eating. For all I know, he could be skin and bones."

"It's been three days. I think he's fine."

"Well, I just want to be sure." She reached in her bra and

pulled out a roll of cash. "Here, please bring him some soup. I would've asked my assistant, but she left for the day already."

There was a moment of hesitancy, not because I've never done a personal errand for Deirdra, but because this meant going to see Luca. My heart jittered at the thought, but I needed to keep a calm composure.

"Um—okay, so I am just dropping off at the door?"

"Oh! Of course, dear. You don't need to go into his apartment." She slid the money into my hands. "Just leave it at the door and start your weekend early."

• • •

"Turn right at the next light," My GPS spoke through the car speakers.

I peeked back behind the passenger seat. Four different types of soups packed tightly in a box. Why? Because Deirdra didn't specify which soup she wanted me to pick up, just slid me cash and texted an address.

My eyes returned to the road, though I didn't have to be super careful. I was in the most coveted part of the city. It was the land of BMW's, Land Rovers, and Mercedes. Where women dressed in athletic wear were either going to Pilates or play tennis, and men wore outerwear vests over their dress shirts to go to the office. *Yes, that part.*

My 2008 Jeep stuck out like a guest who wore jeans to a formal wedding. Parking was almost impossible, but I managed to squished my car between a Porsche and a Lincoln.

"Hello," the doorman greeted. "How can I help you?"

"Hello, I'm visiting suite 621."

"Let me announce your arrival to Mr. Lontern. What's your name?"

"Olivia Kaddel." I strolled around the lobby and admired the fine displays of art while I waited.

"Good evening, Mr. Lontern," I heard him say. "Yes, Olivia Kaddel here for you," he continued. "Yes, sir, Olivia Kaddel. I am certain."

He hung up the phone and gave me a thumbs up. "You're good to go. Elevators are to your left."

The elevator opened to a well-decorated hallway with four doors. Luca's door was the one down the hall. With the only available body part I had, I pressed the doorbell with my forehead and waited until the door swung open.

A puzzled Luca stood across from me, dressed in fitted a black henley and grey sweatpants, with hair still damp from a recent shower.

"You're here?" he asked. "Why?"

"Your aunt thought you were skin and bones, so I brought you soup. Broccoli and cheddar, tomato, lentil, and chicken noodle."

The pain of holding four sixteen-ounce soups for so long was taking a toll on my arms. I was barely able to lift it to him without trembling.

Luca realized. "Here, let me take that. Please come in."

I had no intention of walking into the apartment, but my feet didn't get the memo and walked over the threshold.

Simple. His apartment was simple and decorated in neutral tones. A love seat, an armchair, a standard kitchen and a dining table that sat four. There was a hallway, which I presume had a bathroom and bedroom.

"Surprised?" He studied me from the kitchen. "I told you before, I can read your face."

"Who decorated your apartment?" I went straight to the point.

"Myself, who else would decorate my apartment?" he asked. He pulled out two bowls and poured soup into each. The smell of chicken noodle drew me closer to the kitchen island.

"Your aunt has an assistant for everything, so I assumed you'd be the same."

He passed me the bowl with a spoon in it and smiled. "Maybe you just assume too much, Olivia."

I took a sip of broth and savored the saltiness of the chicken. "Hmm, well sometimes I'm right."

The soup was too good not to take another spoonful and then another. It wasn't until my spoon finally scraped the bottom of the bowl that I looked up to see Luca's emotionless face staring at me. My gaze dropped down to his bowl. It had barely been touched.

"Were you watching me this entire time?

"You were entertaining," he answered.

Heat rushed to my face. I devoured the soup in under five minutes, probably resembling a child who hadn't eaten in ages.

My darker complexion had no chance against my embarrassment. I kept my gaze on his marble countertop. "Um sorry, I usually have manners. I promise I do."

"I am not judging you." He paused to swirl his spoon in the bowl now avoiding my stare. "I do enjoy your company."

I couldn't tell if he was teasing me or not. His soft hazel eyes still hadn't returned to mine, his nose created a shadow over his mouth which I couldn't tell if it was a smile or frown.

"Your aunt said you had a fever. Did you have the flu?"

"It was an upper respiratory infection with a mid-grade fever. The fever broke yesterday, but I took another sick day to regain some strength."

My head angled left to get a better look at his drained complexion. I'd never seen him this colorless before.

"So, how do you feel today?"

"Better enough to take a much needed shower, but even that exhausted me. Anyway, you should go." He sluggishly walked into the living room, and dropped himself on the sofa face-first. "I'm getting better, but you should still keep your distance."

Normal people would've picked up their belongings and left, not wanting to catch any tail end of an upper respiratory infection, but once again my body betrayed me. A stack of tea bags were stashed in the corner next to an electric tea kettle. Lemon tea with honey always hits the spot after fighting an infection. I heated the water up and grabbed a tea bag, one that preferably had lemon, but there was no honey in his cabinets.

Who doesn't have honey in their home? It's every kitchen's staple. *Okay, Olivia, think.* I think I might've seen—I opened a lower cabinet where Luca stored his onions, potatoes, and—perfect. Ginger!

I shaved some ginger in the tea and stirred. From the kitchen, my eyes ventured back to Luca, whose face no longer kissed the couch but now was watching me with a raised eyebrow. He's probably going to hate this, but it's his fault for not having honey.

The thought of seeing his face tighten from a sip of oversaturated lemon ginger tea amused me more than it should, so I walked it over to him.

I sat down and drew the tea closer to his lips. The closer I leaned in to him the more he leaned back, with a face more perplexed than before.

"It's not going to kill you." I rolled my eyes.

"Then why were you smiling?"

"Oh, you saw that." I paused. "Don't worry, it means nothing." I offered him the tea again. "I need you to get better so you can get back to work on Monday. I don't need to be swamped with work anymore."

Luca's eyes softened at my admission. He took the tea and sipped small amounts at a time. "Should I make Monday a remote day? Would that relieve your stress?"

I couldn't help but scoff. "Remote day? At BSG?"

"You don't believe in remote days? I need to convert you then."

"Tsk." I crossed my legs. "I'm not an unbeliever, but your aunt is."

"Let me handle that. The company is just as much as mine as it is hers." He took more sips. "Anyway, thank you."

"You're welcome. I know the ginger is strong, but that's all—"

"Not for the tea."

"Oh, right." I nodded. "For covering for you."

"But for the tea as well," he added, before taking longer sips. The ginger didn't bother him as much as I thought it would.

"It helps," he murmured from his cup before setting it down. "Where did you learn how to make it?"

"My mom used to make it when—Sorry, one moment." I reached for my phone, which had been vibrating in my pocket since I sat down.

Mom: Dad's in the hospital again.

The text brought a slew of thoughts to the forefront of my mind.

Why was he in the hospital again? I thought he was improving with the medication? I think I might have to visit them soon, but there is so much to do at work right now. When will I have the time?

"What's wrong?" Luca asked.

His question pulled me out of my thoughts. "Umm." I slid my phone back into my pocket and shook my head. "It's just family stuff."

He didn't ask after that, but I knew he wanted to. His gaze wouldn't leave my pocket where my phone hid.

I, on the other hand, needed to steady my nerves. This week

had taken me by surprise, and after that text, a wave of uneasiness was emerging. I wrapped my arms around my stomach, knowing what was coming—the cramps.

"Olivia," Luca spoke loudly.

The strength in his voice had startled me. I hadn't expected his director's voice, especially not after three days of being sick.

"Luca," I answered, softly.

"Please talk to me this time." He scooted closer, his knee brushing up against mine. His arm rested on the ledge of the sofa behind my back but still gave me enough room for space. Sara would screech at this moment—any girl would, but Luca wasn't making a move; his eyes pleaded with me to let him into my world.

This week had been too long, and I was too tired to keep up the persona. I needed something, someone to lean on just for a moment.

My lips trembled as I struggled to find the words.

"Luca I-I'm tired, and—" I sighed. "I need to rest."

"Then rest," he whispered.

His words gave me permission to do what I've been wanting to do for a while now. My head leaned forward and crashed on his chest. At once, my body curled in a ball as I leaned more into him. He smelled like himself, like cedar and soap. His body was generous, and I appreciated the shared warmth.

Luca snaked his large arms around my back. My body began to slide down with all the movement, but he pulled me back and secured me against his chest.

I looked over at a mirror hanging on the wall. It captured the perfect angle of Luca and me, and it also gave me the opportunity to look at him without breaking the embrace. His defined chin rested on the top of my head. His arms locked safely around me, and his eyes closed, giving no indication of when they would open.

We sat there in silence together, on his sofa. For how long, I don't know. I hadn't realized that the sun, which earlier had been peeking through the blinds, was now descending, and the stomach cramps had long disappeared. I closed my eyes and listened to his heartbeat, which was evenly paced and beautifully rhythmical.

We could've been there for an hour or two; I'd have no clue. There was no urge to check my phone, no one to rush home to.

"Luca," I whispered.

"Yes, Olivia?" His deep voice brought shivers down my back.

I lifted my head to meet his gaze. I don't know what it was about the evening that gave Luca the softest features. "Are you doing okay? I've pinned you here for a while now."

"Hmm," he hummed.

I could feel him shifting underneath me until we were sitting upright again.

"What is it?" I frowned, saddened that the embrace was broken.

"I want to—" his hand stretched out to my face but stopped. He sighed heavily, letting out his frustrations without saying them.

My hand reached over to take hold of his hand, to delicately travel my fingers down the crevice of his knuckles, and between his fingers until we were interlocked. Still, he didn't continue. Something was holding him back.

"Am I making you uncomfortable?"

He tilted his head, offended. "No, it's not that at all." Finally, he inched in closer but stopped a hair's breadth from my mouth.

My lips trembled. "Please continue."

"I could make you sick," he murmured, his thumb brushed along my cheek. "And I never forgive myself."

He meant it, that he'd hate himself. And while I despised

being sick, it was the genuine sweetness of Luca that ignited the moment.

"Luca, I have worked at BSG for six years. I have enough days for you to keep me sick for months."

And like that, his supple lips greeted mine, massaging slowly and steadily. My hands, having nowhere to go, dropped down to his thighs and rested there. The more his lips moved against mine, the weaker I became, sighing into the kiss. I was losing stamina, and he felt it. His left hand cupped my chin, bringing it back to its original position, while his other hand crawled into my curly hair, supporting my head. Even after being sick for three days, he still had more strength than me.

Luca slipped into the lead effortlessly. He was the conductor, and I was the orchestra. He created a tempo between us, making sure we were in rhythm with each other. When it was time to deepen our kiss, he added subtle pressure, but his last push was firm and my mouth opened.

We paused. He hadn't expected it, and neither had I, for I had gone ahead of our song.

The kiss had melted me into a puddle, and I had little energy to apologize for my unexpected advancement. "Sorry, Luca," I uttered in a small voice.

He smiled. "Why do you torture me, Olivia?" He parted his lips to match mine and pressed into me.

Inside his mouth was new land. Uncharted territory, ready to be conquered by my tongue. But he had gotten into my land first; his warm tongue scoped the landscape of my mouth.

He kept going until there was an unexpected pause. He finally came up, but only an inch or so away from me. I grunted at the interruption.

With a gentle smile, he moved a strand of hair away from my eyes and behind my ear. "We need air, Olivia," he panted.

"Air is overrated."

"Your lips are red," he observed. He brushed them lightly with his finger as if he could heal them. "I'm sorry, I was too eager."

"We've been apart for days, we're both eager," I admitted.

"Hmm..." He picked up my right hand and gave it a tender kiss. "I'll be sure never to do that again."

I watched him. He held my hand like delicate china, and my heart lightened at the sight. It had been a while since any man had touched me like that—perhaps ever.

I tried to savor the moment, knowing it couldn't last. Guilt settled in my stomach almost immediately. By the time the kiss ended, I knew it was already over for me.

Luca's eyebrows pinched together. "What's the matter?"

"Nothing."

He knew me too well to give up. He lifted my chin with two fingers so that I meet his gaze.

I gave in. "You can report me to HR on Monday." I exclaimed. "I'm not sure how long they will give me, but hopefully by the end of the quarter, if I'm lucky."

"That's what you were worried about? Olivia, you are so far from that, that shouldn't even cross your mind."

"You don't get it!" My eyes blurred with tears. "Things always feel good at the moment until it ends." I got up to find my bag, I needed to get out of here and quick. Luca followed.

"Oliva," he called.

I turned around, my voice on the brink of breaking. "No, people like you will never get it!"

"Olivia," he called again, but I continued to gather my things. I didn't need to be here any longer than I already had been. The damage was done.

"Olivia. Look. At. Me." His voice grew louder.

I took a deep breath and turned around to meet him."Listen, I am a Black woman who went over to her boss's house to deliver soup, not to make out with him on his sofa. I've worked hard to get where I am. Everything I have I had to struggle for." Warm tears race down my cheeks onto the hardwood floor. "All my life, I had to work to get a tenth of what you can get in a moment, and I blew it in one evening. I am so stupid." I picked up my things and ran out the door.

11

Monday was a remote day. He kept his promise. The email was sent Sunday afternoon around four p.m. If only I could witness the employees' faces as they sat at home with their golden retrievers laying on their lap and feet up. They'd opened their laptop to an unexpected email for their first ever remote day. I wondered how he pull it off. The Deirdra I know would wear a polyester dress before ever committing to a work from home day. But this was Luca we were talking about. Deirdra had no children, so I suppose her beloved nephew Luca could influence her decisions any way he liked.

I'd be lying if I didn't admit how backwards I felt. My alarm went off at its usual time, seven a.m. I reached over to shut it off, knocking my lamp over in the process. I sat up on my bed and looked around my poorly-lit room. My cat repositioned himself on my legs, annoyed that I had disturbed his sleep.

I leaned down and kissed his furry head. "Lucky for you. You'll have me all day. I'm not leaving."

It was as if Link could understand English—he lifted his head and greeted me with a nose kiss, then meowed happily.

My feet tiptoed into the bathroom, not wanting to fully

place my skin on the icy tile floor, and stopped in front of the mirror. Clumps of day-old mascara glued my eyelashes together. The sad thing was I didn't go out yesterday, I was just practicing a new makeup look. Sara would jump for joy knowing I was exploring the world of makeup, but I hadn't told her yet. Maybe it was my pride,knowing she was right, and that I enjoyed doing makeup. There was something oddly satisfying about mixing colors, manipulating depth, and adding warmth to my face. All that was left was remembering to wash it off before bed.

A steamy shower was good enough to melt the dried mascara off. I closed my eyes as the hot droplets pounded against my face. I could feel my straight hair revert under the water into loose spirals. The best part was, there was no need to rush, no traffic to race against, no meeting demanding my time.

Soft meows woke me up from my daydream. I pulled the shower curtain back to reveal the orange face staring back at me.

"Linky, I know it's weird that I'm still here, but don't be anxious." I reached down to pet him, but he shrieked from my wet hands and ran away.

I dried off and slipped on a pair of yoga pants and a Linkin Park t-shirt. As for my hair, I left it untouched and wet, free to move as it pleased, unbothered by my usual routine.

The last piece of my avocado toast was halfway into my mouth when my phone buzzed.

One message from Group Chat: People I See Too Often

Sara: Miss you guys.

Oscar: You saw us on Friday.

Sara: Ugh my manager sent me a list of things to accomplish by EOD. Olivia, why can't managers just let us be?!!

I laughed knowing that it was because some BSG employees can't be trusted at home, like her. Yesterday, Luca sent a follow-up email to all managers, requesting a list of tasks for every department. *A remote day doesn't mean a free day,* he concluded firmly.

Oscar: I got a list too, and trust me, mine is long.

Olivia: Hey, look at it this way, at least you two are in the comfort of your own home. Just remember to check in with your team via Slack. And sorry Oscar for the long list, whatever you don't get done, I can finish on my end.

Sara: There's her manager voice again.

Oscar: LOL, I can hear it in her text. She can't help herself.

I put the phone aside and knew their jokes were harmless. It was something I didn't mind, and it was inevitable considering I was the only manager in the friend group. I took some time reviewing Oscar's workload, making sure it was actually achievable on his end.

I wasn't sure he could handle the list I'd made for him, but Deirdra had been clear—he needed to be stretched more. It was laughable since I was getting stretched more, yet still passed over for the director position.

Lunch at home was also a new experience for me. I ran a lap around the neighborhood, then headed inside for a grilled cheese with a side salad. There was even some time for a power nap with Link.

"Nine New Emails," my laptop notified from the living room. I walked over with a cup of freshly brewed tea in my hand. Each email varied in urgency, but I got it all done, and without feeling stressed by the end of it.

The last email came in at 4:57 p.m.:

HELLO,

I hope everyone enjoyed their remote day. It's time to sign off. No overtime is allowed on remote days unless approved by me or Deirdra. Enjoy your evening and see you tomorrow.

Luca Lontern

Director of Operations

Business Solutions Group

I closed my laptop. He said no overtime unless approved by him or Deirdra. So, that's it, then. *God, did that feel good. To not only be physically signed off, but mentally as well.*

I leaned against the wall and looked at my clock, "5:00". Link rubbed himself against my leg and meowed, begging for the attention he's had all day.

"Let's eat dinner," I said to him.

He followed me into the kitchen, where I pulled out my mom's recipe book that she let me borrow a year ago. It was time to do something different other than my usual boring Chicken Alfredo.

Let's see here. I flipped page after page until I found something colorful enough that caught my eye. "Huh, ricotta and basil crepe manicotti." I threw on my apron and within forty-five minutes I was sitting across a hard-earned meal.

"Bon appétit," I said to Link, who already headed deep into his Fancy Feast dinner.

Did I look pathetic as a thirty-one-year-old eating dinner alone with her cat? Maybe. The last time I had dinner with a man was Luca on Friday, and the time before that was Luca when we stayed late together, and time before was again, Luca.

Eating with Luca was enjoyable; it's always been nice, I guess. He was good company and someone I looked forward to seeing. I twirled my fork around the remaining bites of my pasta and wondered what he was up to. We hadn't communicated since our forbidden lip lock on Friday, unless you're counting work email from today.

Guilt from our interaction still lingered in my gut. Apology was needed, specifically on my end. I picked up my phone and scrolled down my contacts until I reached "Job Stealer," opened the message, and began drafting.

"Hey, work was quiet today and—" No, no, that wasn't going to work. I backspaced and tried again.

"So, about last Friday—" No, that's too straight to the point. I backspaced again. Why can't I get this right? I moved over to the living room and relaxed down on the couch.

Okay, Olivia, just write what comes naturally. I took a deep breath and tapped.

"Luca, I miss you and I'm sorry." I stared at the words that came out of me, then hit backspace again.

"Ahh!" I moaned and dropped my phone onto the floor, waking up Link from his slumber.

"Meow," Link cried out to me.

"No, it's not feeding time again. I just made a mess of things. That's all." I turned to look at him. "Do you think I should call Sara? You know she's an expert at these things."

Link licked his lips.

"Yeah, I agree. A thirty-year-old should know how to navigate the relationships in her life without needing her best friend all the time."

Link didn't understand English, but he understood love. He jumped on the sofa and walked on my legs until he reached my back. I tried not to cringe as his nails punctured through my shirt and into my skin, but when he reached his ideal spot, he laid down in a typical cat loaf position.

I smiled knowing he'd expect an evening treat in exchange for this act of love, but I appreciated the gesture anyway.

• • •

"Good morning Olivia," Dale said with an ear-to-ear grin. His voice was perkier than usual.

"Morning Dale, how was your Monday?"

"Quiet," he stretched. "Especially with that remote day yesterday. By the way, what did we do to deserve that? It came out of nowhere."

I shrugged, though I knew exactly why it happened. *Me.*

"Well, it looks like it was a great call. Work morale seems high this morning."

Dale wasn't wrong. The lobby was bustling with laughter and good spirits. Employees were arriving as early as I was, and it wasn't even nine yet. Then I spotted him. Luca, a magnet as always, attracting employees to him as if they were random pieces of metal.

Normally, I would dodge him the best I could. Then he'd eventually catch me with his hazel eyes, though I never knew how he did it amongst the swarm of arriving employees.

Except this time, he didn't. I've been standing next to Dale for some time now, and he didn't even spare me a look.

"Are you okay?" Dale asked.

"Huh?"

"You seem—distant. That's not like you." He frowned.

I blinked a few times to wake myself up. "Yeah, just a little more tired than usual I guess."

Dale glanced at Luca, then turned back to me. "Uh-huh, tired. Right."

"I gotta get going, see ya."

My eyes stayed glued on Luca as I passed through the gate. For sure this time he would notice me. He didn't.

I arrived at my cubicle and opened my laptop. My heart leaped when I saw:

"New Message from Luca"

"Hope you enjoyed your remote day yesterday. Our Monday morning meeting is rescheduled for today at 10. See you then. - Luca."

Right, this wasn't a personal message, every manager was cc'd on it. The elevator dinged. Immediately, I popped up out of my cubicle, but it was only my team.

"Oh! Good morning, Olivia," Alexis said as she walked out.

"Good morning, Alexis."

"Hey, Olivia."

I swung around to see Japhet waving from the hallway.

"Hey, Japhet." I forced a smile and sank back down to my office chair.

Oscar walked in. "Morning, boss."

"Morin'." I swiveled around to him. "How was your remote day?"

"Wonderful!" he exclaimed. "And how was yours? After last week, you out of all people needed one."

"Agreed," I nodded. "Link and I never spent that much time together on a weekday, but I think it threw his schedule off. Hey! Are you listening?"

But Oscar was distracted. He had been peeking above my cubicle waving.

"Who are you waving at?"

"Luca," he answered. "He just came up."

His name triggered a sigh in me.

"What's wrong?" Oscar asked. "What, I can't say hi to Luca?"

"No, no. Come with me," I pulled him to the secluded stairwell, where I was sure no one would hear us. "I have to tell you something."

Oscar raised a brow. "Please do, because you're acting weird."

"Okay, here it goes." I took a deep breath. "I kissed Luca."

"No, you didn't." He rolled his eyes. "What's really going on?"

"Excuse me?" I stepped back surprised that he didn't believe me. "Oscar Raúl Bedonalez."

Oscar's eyes stretched open. I had used his full name. He knew I was serious.

"Wait, what!" He stepped back in shock, almost tripping on himself, but I caught him.

"Shh." I calmed him. "Keep your voice down."

Oscar starred as he processed the news. I glanced at his chest, which rose up and down. Good, he was still breathing, but just a little shaken.

"Sorry, I just didn't expect that from you. Tell me what happened!"

I leaned against the wall to recall the events on that eventful Friday evening. "Well, Deirdra needed me to drop off food for Luca. So, I did, then I saw him and we started catching up about things. Then I got a message from my mom saying my dad was back at the hospital, then—then Luca was holding me. He was holding me for a while, and it just happened."

Oscar kept silent, which I expected since he wasn't like Sara. He was more level-headed, which is why I told him first. I needed someone who was level-headed about the situation, but he hadn't said anything yet, so I continued.

"And well, the kiss wasn't just a peck. It was long, and it kept going."

"So, it was mutual?"

"Very."

Oscar nodded. "So, he wasn't taking advantage of you at all?"

"No," I clarified. "Luca isn't like that. He's different. He's gentle and very kind. He's—he's just," I took a deep breath, my body was finally able to relax.

"I get it," Oscar said.

"So, afterwards we had a disagreement on how to go about the kiss, and I left on a sour note. So, that's where I'm at now. What should I do?"

"You know what you need to do," he said blatantly. "Talk to him."

I moaned. "What do I say? I suck at this."

It was as if the second I said it, the door flung open. Luca held it open with his forearm while his attention was solely on Oscar.

I open my mouth to say hello "Hi, Luc—"

"Oscar," Luca cut me off. "Can you grant me access to the final report that you did for that client last week?"

"Yes sir," Oscar walked around me to follow him out. I followed them back to our desks. Luca hung over Oscar's cubicle wall while Oscar pulled up the report. They joked about the weekend and various sports while I scrolled through my computer, wanting to join in but not feeling welcomed.

"Thanks Oscar," Luca walked away, and I was able to return to our conversation.

"Awkward," Oscar noted.

"I know. That's what I was afraid of."

"Luca didn't even acknowledge you. Which is out of his nature." Oscar thought. "Was the disagreement really that bad? Wait, did you run out on him?"

"Umm."

"Olivia," Oscar crossed his arms as my father used to do. "You know, you really need to stop doing that. Now you have to face the consequences."

It was 9:50 and I arrived at our meeting room early enough to pull Luca aside to talk to him. He sat at the center with just his laptop, focused in while he typed away.

"Hey, Luca," I walked in closer. "Could we chat for a quick moment?"

He didn't bother looking up, instead kept his eyes glued to his laptop. "Is this important? Could we talk about it later?"

A sudden sadness engulfed my chest. "That's fine, I took my seat at the table and waited as others trickled in.

A looming noise was heard down the hall, moments later Connor burst into the conference room. "Aye! Mornin'! Lookin' good, Robin Hood!" he sang, handing out shoulder slaps like party favors.

The rest of the management followed, some with their voices on max volume, some scrolling on their phone, and some coming in just after ten with a Starbucks coffee in hand.

Luca kept a keen eye on the door, scribbling something every time another manager appeared. Each note came after a glance at his Rolex, like clockwork—literally. It wasn't before long for people to catch on, and when they did, coffee mysteriously vanished, phones went face-down, and laptops sprang open.

After the last manager arrived. He shut the door and wrote the numbers "10:16" in red on the white board.

He slid his hands into his pockets. "Ten sixteen," he read off the board. "That's the time we're starting. This meeting is supposed to be one hour, and many of you stole sixteen minutes from the group, which means I'm taking sixteen minutes of your time. Remember that next time you prioritize your caffeine and tardiness." He opened his laptop. "Let's begin, Employee Expectation..."

Luca was forward with all his points, leaving little room for questions or opposition. His tone was stronger for this meeting, and even though he wasn't the only male in the room, he made sure to exercise his alpha male energy.

He flipped up his wrist one last time. "11:16," he read. "That concludes the end of the meeting. Remember, reports are expected in my inbox by Friday two p.m. sharp. Dismissed."

There were no lingering conversations or last-minute remarks. Like freshly reprimanded students, we sprang out of the seats and exited the room in a straight line.

"Hold the elevator for me," I called out to Connor.

He held his hand out and I squeezed in. Every manager was

in the elevator, meaning no one wanted to be in the room with Luca.

"Thanks," I said.

"No problem." Connor nodded as he flipped through his notes from the meeting. "Crazy meeting, huh? Reports, expenses, tracking employee work progress. Did we do something wrong? Because it seemed that he was bringing down the hammer on us."

"He was different this time around," Rasheed agreed.

"Yeah, I thought he was the chill boss." Connor scoffed and turned to me. "What's gotten into him anyway? Do you know anything?"

I pointed to myself. "Are you asking me?"

"Yeah, you work with him the most. Surely you must know why he's on edge today."

Everyone fell silent, waiting for my answer. I bit my lip, trying to figure out a way out of this one.

I shrugged. "I mean, he was absent most of last week. He has a lot to catch up on, so he's probably feeling it today."

Ding. "That's my floor. Good luck, guys." I sped out of the elevator to avoid any more questions and headed straight for my desk.

I turned the corner and spotted Sara chatting carefree to Oscar. "Sara," I whispered. "You need to go back down to your department. Luca is not in a mood today."

Sara looked at me strangely. "Really? You're the third person who's told me that."

Oscar nodded. "And I'll be the fourth. Luca isn't playing games. Go back to work."

She waved him off. "Everyone is being overdramatic. This is Luca we're talking about. Why are you two acting so weird?" She folded her arms and zeroed in on me. "Especially you, Olivia. What's going on?"

"Have you not told her yet?" Oscar asked me.

"Told me what?!" Sara pestered more.

"No," I answered in a low voice. "This is not the time and—"

"Hey." Luca came up from behind. "What are you guys working on?"

"Uhh." Sara looked back and forth between Oscar and me. She, out of the three of us, needed to make the best excuse since this was not on her department.

"We—huh we're just talking about lunch plans."

"You're using company time to talk about lunch plans?"

"Well..." Sara began.

"Also, it's 11:22, Lunch can't be taken any earlier than noon unless approved by your manager. Did Connor approve you?"

"No."

He turned to me abruptly, daring eyes stared into me. "So, did Olivia approve?"

"No, I'm not her manager," I answered quickly.

"Hmm," he looked at his watch and cleared his throat. "I know me and Olivia have tons of work to do, and I assigned some work to Oscar this morning. Do you need something to work on Sara, or should I—"

"Nope." She grabbed her phone and got ready to leave. "I've got presentations, conference calls and—oh my—so much to do in the sales department." She snuck behind Luca, out of his line of sight, and turned around. "Oh my gosh!" She mouthed to me. "He is mean!"

Oscar nudged me on the side, hinting that I should look ahead.

I return my attention to the towering man that hadn't visually let go of me. Luca kept a straight face through it all. I couldn't tell if he was truly mad at us or if he was just reminding us to get back to work.

"Olivia, a word in my office," Luca said.

"Good luck," I could hear Oscar whisper behind.

I sighed and followed him down the hall.

"Ooooh…" The peeping employees murmured as they spied.

"Olivia is in trouble?"

"What do you think she did?"

Luca waited until I fully entered the room before closing the door behind me, making the situation even more dramatic.

I did my best to keep calm and smile, but I was far from the smiling mood. Why did he have to make a scene like that? He could've pulled Sara aside and talked to her privately about her excessive visitation with me. He could just talk to me after our meeting instead of calling me into his office like some defiant high school student.

My body plunged into his stiff leather chair. He took his seat and scooted in. I guess he wanted this to be formal.

"Olivia," he began.

"That was unnecessary," I cut him off. "You should've said that to her in private, and why are you being so rough today? Everyone is working and morale is high."

"I am not being rough," he said bluntly. "If someone is upset at the way I manage it's because I'm finally setting a standard, and they didn't expect that."

"You're not getting it." I scooted closer to the edge of my seat. "Listen, we all work hard."

"*You* work hard," he corrected.

"My colleagues too," I argued back. "You can't just bring the hammer down on them just because of me."

That caught his attention. His brow pinched together, and his jaw clenched. "Because of you?" His voice peaked.

"Yes." My voice lowered.

"Olivia, this is not about you." He paused. "And let me make this clear, this is not about us." He said it both loudly and slowly.

That alone pushed me to the edge. "Don't talk to me like I'm a child. Deirdra talks to me like that, and I don't need another member from the Lontern/Scottfield family doing the same thing."

"I am not, but I need you to understand, especially because I know you're not going to believe me," he countered.

"I don't believe you because it feels like you're making this about us, and you know I'm going to be questioned about it. People have already started to ask."

"By who?!" His voice heightened, which proved my point.

"This is what I am saying! I shouldn't get privileges! I hate privilege!"

"No, that's not what I meant," he grunted. "I mean, I'm frustrated but that's not—" He sighed. "Fine. If you feel like you're getting special treatment, we'll stop."

It felt like the wind was knocked out of me when he said that. I knew what it meant, but for some reason I wanted him to explain. "Wait, what do you mean 'stop'?"

"All of it," he answered coldly. "Us."

My heart dropped to my stomach, and stiffness paralyzed my body. I opened my mouth to respond, but my brain couldn't form words.

"Moving forward we'll be professional," he continued.

"Umm." I blinked a couple of times, hoping to return blood flow to my body. "Okay, I guess."

I could've sworn the edge of his mouth tilted downwards. "It's what we want, right?" he said in a whisper.

Once I was finally able to regulate my body, I sat silently across from him. My heart felt like it was just under attack in a way I never thought I'd feel from him.

It was coming—the warm tears building up. I needed to get out here and fast.

"Right, Friday was a mistake."

"No." Luca stood up. "No, I never said that."

I got up and wiped my eyes before a single tear could fall. "Friday was a mistake. Going to that convention was a mistake. *We* are a mistake."

"Olivia, please." He walked around his desk in my direction.

"I need to go, Luca." I opened the door and ran out. Several employees rushed back to their cubicles after pretending not to spying.

"You okay?" Oscar asked at the doorway.

"I'm taking an early lunch." I grabbed my bag and walked out into the dark stairwell. It was a couple of flights down until I'd reach the lobby, but it was fine, I needed the walk.

Once I was safely in my car, away from my toxic workplace, away from nosy employees—and definitely away from Luca—my tears began to fall down one by one until they matched a running faucet. My phone couldn't stop vibrating from the moment I got in. I felt around in my bag for the device and silenced it.

12

It's been a week since our talk. We haven't spoken to each other at all except for this one time on Monday when I needed him to sign something. Sara and Oscar have been joining me for lunch almost every day since Luca "broke up with me" as Sara said. I finally told her what happened between us. At first, she was happy, shocked, and angry all at the same time. Happy that Luca and I kissed, shocked that he and I had so much chemistry these past months, and angry that he ended it.

I checked my to-do list for today; our meeting was still on. It was Luca's and my first meeting since our talk. I requested that we meet in his upstairs office since Oscar told me last week #WhatHappenedBetweenLuca&Olivia was a trending hashtag on Slack for two days. I didn't need a reason for them to have episode two.

On the bright side, Sara's has been in my corner, determined to get me through this. She texted me this morning with some revenge ideas.

Sara: Make sure you wear something hot today for your meeting.

Sara: I left you my Jimmy Choo perfume on your desk. Give yourself some pumps before going in.

Sara: MAKE. HIM. SUFFER.

I look down at my outfit. I wasn't sure if it was Sara's definition of "hot". Actually, I knew it wasn't her definition since it wasn't a deep-plunge blouse with a mini skirt. Instead, it was turtleneck dress with booties.

I snapped a picture and sent it to her. "This is as hot as I'm going to get," I captioned.

I sipped water from my bottle and watched my digital clock. I had about five minutes to get to his upstairs office. I didn't want to tell Sara, but there was a small part of me that wanted to speak to him, and I don't know what for. I told myself it was because once it was done and over with, things should be less awkward between us. Though deep down I knew it wasn't the truth, and so did Oscar.

Oscar's been in my corner too—just a different corner. He encouraged me to make amends with Luca, saying that Luca still watches me from the corner of his eye and asks about me every now and then.

Eleven o'clock on the dot, and right on time. Luca's secretary, Lorraine, let me in. She didn't look the happiest today. I giggled knowing it was because Luca decided to work in his upstairs office, meaning she had to actually work instead of online shop.

I walked into his office expecting to find him in his leather chair. Absorbed in his work, his thick, tapered hair fell to the left as he liked it, his hand veins pulsing as he drafted yet another company email.

Except he wasn't at his desk. An empty chair stood before me. His laptop, however, lay open beside the evergreen notebook he usually carried around. He had to be coming back, but I didn't know when. I should've waited outside with Lorriane, but an open photo album stole my attention. I pretended to scope the room as if I was admiring the various office keepsakes he kept. It was at least more interesting than the downstairs office. When I arrived at the open photo album, I slowed my speed to take a longer look.

A group of fifteen people were positioned near a massive pool. The women were in floppy sun hats, the men were burnt lobsters, and the kids posed in duck floaties. Underneath that picture was one of a well-dressed young boy squatting next to a tombstone. I squinted trying to make out the wording, but all I could distinguish was a quote, "We'll make you proud, Pa." The last picture on the next page was a more recent photo of a dark-haired man in a cap and gown, draped in ropes. One hand held a skinny black book while the other held onto a skinny blonde woman. Both smiled widely, so wide it looked like it hurt, but neither of them looked happy. I picked up the book and studied the picture more closely.

It took me a moment to realize the man was indeed Luca. He did in fact have the same piercing hazel eyes and sharp narrow nose, but his hair was buzzed and something about his expression didn't reflect the Luca that I've known.

"Hey."

His voice startled me and the book dropped out of my hands and onto the floor.

"Shoot." I bent down to pick it up, but a large hand reached for it first. The smell of cedarwood permeated the air.

"Good morning, Luca." I stood up quickly and smoothed my dress. There were in fact no wrinkles in my dress, but I needed to do something to hide my embarrassment. "Sorry, I was just looking—and I saw the book and I—" This was stupid. There was no way to excuse that I was snooping in his office.

I finally forced myself to meet the eye contact I'd been avoiding.

He stepped closer to me, his thick but well-groomed brows tense and his nose scrunched. He didn't look mad, but he was focused. "You what—what were you going to say, Olivia?"

Olivia.

I hadn't heard him say my name in a week. He always managed to say my name in his sentences, especially when he wanted me to answer something.

I could feel myself wanting to lean forward, though any more forward would cause our bodies to meet. My mouth parted as words were ready to come out, though it had nothing to do with the album and everything to do with us.

Wake up, Olivia.

I stepped backwards. "Sorry, the photos caught my attention, but I was out of place. Forgive me."

Luca shook his head. "Oh yeah, the album, that's fine." He slid the book onto the shelf behind him. "Did you bring your laptop?"

"Yes." I held up to him. "Let's get to work."

It neared the one-hour mark, but we didn't accomplish anything. Luca was at his desk flipping through countless folders while I sat on his sofa going through digital files with no prevail.

I closed my laptop and tossed it on the cushion, frustrated. Why was this so difficult? Maybe Luca was making headway on his end. I glanced up to see a frustrated Luca looking back at me. We were both doomed.

I stood up and walked over to him. "When is our board-member meeting?"

He flipped open his notebook. "Twenty-seven days."

I moaned and leaned against the wall behind him. He turned his chair to face me.

"This is not looking good for either of us," I finally said. "I am going to get fired. My bills will not get paid. I am going to be kicked out of my apartment, and then me and my cat Link will live in my car for the foreseeable future, along with the goldfish I won from the city carnival."

"Those goldfish don't live long anyway."

"Not if you don't condition your water. Mine is six years old."

"Seriously?!"

"Yes, but let's get back to the matter at hand. What are we going to do about this project?"

We stared silently at each other. We knew the answer all along. It would take full cooperation between the two of us to work together and do the one thing we'd both been avoiding—talking to each other.

He grabbed his laptop and walked over to the sofa. "Come sit with me, Olivia."

I joined him on the sofa and opened my laptop, "What do you want to do?"

"Read me the parts you feel are important, and I'll format them into subpoints; then we'll build from there. If we can get the skeleton of the presentation together, we should be okay. Then, we'll add in the body parts in the coming weeks."

It was nearing three p.m. and I was still in Luca's office. My hair was tossed in a sloppy bun and my booties, kicked off, and somewhere on the floor. We'd worked nonstop since noon. We were afraid that any break past ten minutes would cause us to lose our momentum.

"And that's it." Luca's eyes scanned across the screen several times making sure we were indeed satisfied. "All we need now is to confirm our data for slide eight, but we don't have those records here."

"That was a crazy year for BSG," I recalled. "We store those records in the archive room. I can go check."

"Wait," Luca hand grazed my wrist, causing me to stop.

"Is there something else?"

"No, it's not that." He stood up, his brows pinched together. "Um, I just wanted to check on how you were doing with everything. I know you tend to pack on the duties, but I also don't want you to burn out."

I pointed at myself, confused about where this was coming from. "Me? You don't want *me* to burn out?"

He scratched his head and briefly looked out the window. "Well, I don't want any of my employees to burn out, I mean."

"Of course, I will be mindful. Give me a few minutes to fetch that box of files."

I hurried out of his office and back down to my floor. Lance, our archive administrator, was out on vacation, but Oscar knew the archive room like the back of his hand. I was sure that he'd be able to help me.

"Hey." I knocked on his cubicle.

Oscar turned around with a puzzled face and a phone attached to his ear.

"Oh, sorry," I whispered. "I didn't know that you were on a call."

Oscar held the phone away from his ear. "It's okay, the client put me on hold. What's up?"

"I need to get hold of our annual results from two years ago."

Oscar made a face. "Yuck, that year was a mess for BSG."

"I know, it gives me nightmares 'til this day, but it's part of my and Luca's presentation. Do you happen to know where I can find the archive?"

"Well, you can find all of that in the archive room, top shelf, most likely in aisle twelve, but the bookshelves are quite tall. You're going to need a ladder, and I wouldn't recommend climbing anything with those babies." He pointed at my feet.

"You mean my booties."

"Yes. Listen, I can help you after this call if you'd like."

"Thanks, but I can handle it," I assured him and headed to the archive room.

Dark, dusty, and creepy. I hated everything about this room, which is why I always requested Oscar to fetch things for me.

I opened my phone to shoot Luca a quick text. "Sorry it's taking so long, but I'm grabbing the folders now and I'll be back soon."

The light sensor detected my presence and switched on. Towering bookshelves lined neatly the room. Oscar wasn't kidding about needing a ladder.

I pulled the rolling ladder from the corner and guided it to aisle twelve. I peered up at the daunting task, and held on to the wobbly ladder; fear settled in.

Just don't think about it. Take one step at a time.

What should've been a fifteen-second climb took me three minutes with two additional pep talks, but I made it. I pulled out the first box my hands could reach and shuffled through the folders. It was a tedious task, but I knew exactly what I was looking for. It wasn't until the third box that my patience paid off.

This was it! I pulled out the single manilla folder and descended down. Oscar would be so proud of me. And Luca— oh my—

I missed the sixth step coming down and landed on my left ankle on the floor. I never thought I'd hear the day when my ankle could make a cracking sound, but it did, and the pain was immediate.

"Ow, ow," I panted in agony, feeling like someone pounded a hammer against my ankle. Judging by the pain, there was no way I was going to be able to stand on my feet, but maybe I could at least sit up.

I attempted to lift my body up with the help of my hands but immediately stopped as another twinge of pain shot through my wrist.

I turned my palm over to see a darkened bruise forming on my wrist. I was stuck here lying on the floor. My phone must've slid somewhere after the fall because it was no longer in my pocket.

I tried searching for it, but my lack of body movement caused the lights to switch off. I was in pain, alone, and in the dark, three things that when, combined together, triggered a wave of tears.

The only good thing was that no one was here to witness me crying. It wasn't the first time BSG brought me to this point, but it seemed lately that every week posed another trial to overcome, and I was tired of it.

After what seemed like a much-needed cry, I contemplated shouting for help, but who would hear me? No one, with the exception of Lance, who was currently on vacation. It was only on occasion that a disgruntled employee would venture down here by the request of the manager, like Oscar.

A soft jingle resonated from the left side of the room, and my heart jumped as I glanced around hoping this was a sign from God. With my uninjured wrist, I slowly crawled around in the darkness. Of course, that wasn't enough to trigger the light sensor, but it was all I could do for now. The ringing stopped, and I figured my phone had gone to voicemail. I immediately hated myself for turning off voice command, otherwise I'd tell my phone to call for help.

The phone rang a second time, but by this time I was out of both breath and resilience. I closed my eyes and wished I was anywhere but here. I was instead on green grass on a picnic blanket sounded by fields of flowers and the warm rays of a mid-spring sun. Next to me sat a man with the sought-after height of Luca, the captivating smile of Luca, and of course the enchanting eyes of Luca. He snaked his arm around my waist like Luca did during our cocktail night and whispered into my ear.

"Olivia," he'd say.

"Hmm?" I'd turned to him.

"Olivia," he said louder. "Olivia, are you okay?"

He shook me violently, ruining our sweet moment.

"Why are you shaking me, Luca?" I moaned.

"I'm not Luca," the voice said louder.

"I'll pour some water on her." I heard a different voice say. "Maybe she'll wake up."

Water, what?! I popped open my eyes to see Oscar and Sara staring down at me. Sara had an open bottle of water in her hand, ready to tilt it all over me.

"I am awake! I am awake!" I yelled and jolted up. A sharp pain stung my wrist. "Oh ow-ow-ow."

"So, she did hurt herself," Oscar said to Sara.

"I fell," I said, rubbing my wrist, "off the ladder, and—"

"Do you have a headache?" Sara cut me off and rubbed my head.

"Headache?" I placed my hand on my temple and thought. "No, I don't think so."

Oscar took my arm and placed it over his shoulder to help me up. "We need to get her to the hospital."

"Wait, I can't walk, I hurt my left ankle."

"I can help as well." Sara stood on the opposite side of me, and with their help, I hopped out of the archive room and into the elevator.

"What happened?" Dale rushed over the second we entered the lobby.

"I fell in the archive room," I said in a low voice, "but I'm okay."

"Oh, my dear." He frowned. "Let me get the door for you

guys. Take good care of my Olivia," he shouted out to Sara and Oscar once we got to the parking lot.

We hopped in Oscar's car and within fifteen minutes I was sitting in a stiff, cold wheelchair in the hospital waiting room. Oscar and Sara did their best to distract me with the latest office gossip and new rom com they've been watching.

The nurse called me into my room shortly. Thankfully, the hospital had a two-visitor limit so neither of them had to be left behind. Once I was settled in my bed, it dawned on me that my phone wasn't on me.

"Are you looking for your phone?" Sara said and pulled it out of her pocket. "Found it against the wall, but it didn't survive the fall." She passed it over to me.

I inspected the web-like cracks that now split my screen into three different parts. "Still works though," I smiled as my screen lit up.

Five missed calls. 12 Unread Messages "4:47! Wow, it's that late!" I turned to her. "I'll shoot Connor a message letting him know you are with me. I don't want him to think you left work early."

Sara leaned back on the chair and scrolled on her phone. "No need, I let him know already. He gave me the thumbs up."

I nodded, happy that Connor's chill attitude benefited his employees at times like these. Now to check my messages.

Four missed messages from Luca. "Shoot," I almost dropped my phone for the second time today.

"What?" Oscar became alarmed.

"Luca was waiting for me!" I exclaimed. "He probably thinks I bailed on him."

A nurse pulled the curtain back and peeked in. "Oliva, I'm going to take you to get some x-rays now."

Oscar took my phone out of my hand. "Just worry about yourself right now. I'll let Luca know."

"Thanks guys. I owe you one."

The nurse rolled me out of the room. "You have good friends," she mentioned as she passed me to the x-ray tech.

She wasn't wrong. They were the best work friends one could ever ask for. They've been with me through every up and down during my BSG career and personal life. I'll make it a point to treat them nicely this holiday season.

"All done, Ms. Kaddel." The x-ray tech came back into the room to remove my smock. "The doctor will notify you of your results shortly."

I thanked him, and the nurse rolled me back into my room where I found Sara and Oscar with stunned faces.

"Are you guys okay?" I immediately asked.

Sara chuckled and nudged Oscar. "Tell her."

"Tell me what?!" I was getting anxious.

Oscar passed me my phone. "So, I called Luca..."

Why was he taking so long with this? "You called Luca...and?"

"Let's just say he didn't sound too happy."

"Ugh, probably because he was waiting on those files I was supposed to bring to him." I thought some more. "Or that the two of you brought me to the hospital during work hours."

Sara shook her head in frustration. "She doesn't get it."

"Get what?" I sat up, annoyed.

Oscar settled me back down. "Don't worry, he's on his way now."

That statement didn't settle me at all. I sprang back up. "On his way?! Okay, let me do the talking."

Now, they both were chuckling to each other, but I couldn't be bothered anymore with it. I spent the next few minutes contemplating a compelling story so neither of them would get in trouble.

The nurse pulled back the curtain once more. "Here she is,

Olivia Kaddel." *Please let that be the doctor*. I just wanted my results so we could leave already.

It was in fact not the doctor, but Luca. He had rushed into my room disheveled and somewhat disorientated. His jacket was barely on, his cheeks beet red, and his hair looked like it had been blown out by the salon.

"Are you okay, Olivia?" he asked out breath.

"Are *you* okay—is a better question." I emphasized, hinting at his rapid breathing.

"Why didn't you call me?"

"Because I couldn't find my phone and I—" There was no need to continue; he was not paying attention. His eyes were scanning my body looking for any visible damage.

Sara and Oscar were now in full whisper mode in the corner.

"Luca," I said, hoping to get his attention. "Luca, look at me," I said much stronger. Luca stopped searching and brought his hazel eyes to mine. They were frantic at first, but once they met mine, they softened.

"Are you okay?" he whispered to me in a tired voice.

"A little banged up, but not dead," I assured him.

My answer was enough to relax him, and he smiled half-heartedly.

He glanced up at Sara and Oscar. "Thanks for looking after her. You two are free to go. I'll take over from here."

"Oh, okay." Sara shot me a *what the heck* look. I shrugged my shoulders, not really knowing that was his plan.

Oscar tugged Sara by her arm. "Of course, we'll head out right away. Right Sara?"

"Okay, okay. I'm coming." She gathered her things and they both waved goodbye. Oscar even winked at me.

Once they were gone, my attention returned to Luca, who was fixated on my ankle. I took the free time to finally explain what happened. He nodded slowly, taking it all in. I frequently offered for him to sit down, but he denied my requests, saying he preferred to stand. It was something I was fine with, especially because if he sat down, it would mean he'd stop rubbing my hand, which he'd been subconsciously doing since Sara and Oscar left.

The doctor finally came in and introduced himself. He said I had a minor fracture to my ankle and it would take two weeks to heal. He scheduled me for a follow-up appointment with a physical therapist and gave me a slim brace to put on. I would've been discharged at that point, but Luca then requested I receive an MRI.

That kept us at the hospital for another two hours, but once I was cleared, Luca drove me home.

He parked the car and opened the door for me. Just as I was about to thank him, he scooped me up and secured me in his arms.

Walking over to my door was a breeze from him too, even with cooling night air. "Do you have keys?" he asked.

"Not anymore, my landlord finally installed my code system. 2940 is the code. You think you can enter it without letting me go?

The door clicked open. "Already did." He smirked.

He laid me on my soft velvet sofa. Immediately, I pulled my throw blanket over my body and curled into a ball.

Once Luca took off his jacket and loosened his tie, he sat down next to me. His tired eyes watched my every move, and though he wanted to close them, he fought it with a sweet smile.

Today burnt him out. He could've ended his day at five pm like everyone else, he could've ignored Oscar's phone call and joined in on some happy hour, yet he spent his evening in a hospital with me waiting for MRI results.

"What are you thinking about?" He yawned. "And don't lie to me."

I retreated from my blanket and drew closer to him. "Luca Lontern, you are, without a doubt, a wonderful human being."

That woke him up. In fact, he sat up to get a better look at me. He brought his hand to my forehead. "Maybe we should go back to take another MRI?"

"Fine, but it won't change my opinion of you."

His hand slid down to my mouth and he traced my lips with his finger. "You drive me crazy, Olivia."

The moment was ruined with my constant memory of our agreement last week. "So, last week, we—" I stopped, the word was stuck in my throat, unable to come out.

"Don't," he said. "Let's not repeat it. It clearly doesn't work for us."

He dropped his index finger on my chin and tilted it up so that he had my full attention.

"Plus, you've tortured me enough today, you know that." He rubbed his thumb against my bottom lip. "Let me enjoy this."

I couldn't help but cup his face and feel his stubble chin hair brushing the inside of my palm. It was the first thing I wanted to do after being deprived of him for a week.

"Luca," I whispered. "I've missed you."

Oscar was right, it felt good saying it out loud. It felt so good I needed to say it again.

"I've missed you so much," I breathed, tears spilling as I wrapped him in my arms, holding on as if I could make up for lost time. "Let's not ever do that again."

He dried the corners of my eyes with his thumb, and we reclined deeper into the sofa. His hand stroked my back like it was a guitar. My finger traced the veins running down his arm like they were Braille. His heart was beating heavily against my ear. It was one of the most beautiful things I've experienced, just to hear his heartbeat in the silence of my seven-hundred-square-foot apartment. I wish I could transform the feeling into words, but the English language with all its history, dialects, and splendor couldn't match the feeling brewing in me.

Yes, there were multiple things we could've been doing, like full-on making out, or planning how we were going to go to HR with this, but sitting here secured in each other arms just felt like the right thing to do.

13

The smell of hot, funky cat breath combined with the tickle of whiskers dragged me out of my sleep. I stretched my body and the sharp pain resonating from my ankle quickly reminded me of yesterday's events. I curled back into a ball and wrapped myself into my full-size blanket. The coolness of November had embraced the earth, and I had no intention of getting up. I did, however, search for my phone under the flannel sheets, but it couldn't be found. Then I remembered. I reached over to my side table and opened the drawer to grab my very cracked, very low-battery phone.

Luca had placed it there for me after bringing me to my bed last night. He stashed it in the drawer saying that he knew it would distract me from sleep. He was right. My missed messages had grown from seven to seventeen. I knew most of them had to be Sara, a fraction of those from Oscar, and the rest from my department wondering where I'd disappeared to yesterday. I hadn't decided if I was going to work or not, but I figured I'd see how I felt this morning.

My wrist felt much better, and only when I pressed it hard did it hurt. My ankle, however, made little to no progress. But there was still much to finish with the board member presentation.

My only resort was to hop around while getting ready, preparing my lunch, and feeding my cat. There was no point in even doing makeup or a cute hairstyle. I slipped on a burgundy sweater with a matching skirt and clipped up my hair.

The beep from my front door caught my attention.

"Hello?" I called out, nervous.

"It's Luca," he shouted from afar. He revealed himself from the entryway of the bathroom in his wool coat, striped scarf, and a puzzled expression.

"You look warm," I noted.

"And you look dressed," he noted back. "Why are you dressed by the way?"

"It's Wednesday, and I don't know if you got the memo, but Wednesday is in fact a weekday which means a workday," I said so matter-of-factly. The purpose of my tone was to relax his unusual tension this morning, but I wasn't sure it had worked. His eyebrows were so furrowed they were almost touching. He moved in closer, and I could smell his body soap. He'd used Irish Spring today.

I exhaled heavily; it was the only thing to keep me focused.

"And Mr. Lontern, why are you here?" I teased. "You should be at the office."

He leaned forward and whispered. "I made you breakfast and left it on your table." Soft lips pecked tenderly at the nape of neck. "Breakfast which is supposed to be eaten at home," he came back up to say. "Not at work."

My breath was uneven, and I hadn't even realized his hand was holding me up from falling. This man was killing me.

"What does that mean?" I muttered.

"It means that you're not going to work today." He unclipped my hair and placed the clip on the counter behind me.

Long spirals fell to my shoulders. "But I am—"

"I'm sorry, Olivia. As your boss, it's what I decided."

"How about the Luca who isn't my boss?" I raised a brow. "What does he say?"

He laughed, probably knowing I would spin it around. "He says that you should take the day off and take care of yourself."

I followed him into the living room, where a single bagged breakfast lay on the table. "Are you not eating with me?" I pouted, hoping he would stay a while longer.

He continued to button up his jacket while flashing his smile at me. "I have meetings all day." He ran over and pecked me on my forehead.

"But I'll see you soon. Please eat," he urged before rushing out the door.

• • •

It was another day at home for me—paid, but with no expectation of work. I was finally able to watch that thriller series William told me about. I took a much needed Epsom salt bath, and even started the first five chapters of my new fantasy book.

It was only noon, and I'd already maxed out what I usually did on my days off. I would've found it more enjoyable had I been able to walk around freely. I probably would've gone to the mall—a place I hadn't seen in what felt like ages. It wouldn't have happened anyway. My car was still in the BSG parking lot; my only wish now was that it would start the next time I ignited it.

Maybe it was time to start seriously looking for a new car, but I didn't know where to begin. It was the only car I'd ever had, and it was given to me by my parents. The money was there, but so was my ignorance in purchasing a car—I was a salesman's dream.

I pulled out my laptop. If I had any hope of not being taken advantage of at a dealership, I had to inform myself. The screen lit up, and there laid my unfinished presentation. Looking at it now, we did a considerable amount of work yesterday. We just needed to fix something on this slide and a chart on the other slide, and while I'm at it, I might as well spell check. Before I knew it, an hour had passed and my phone rang.

Incoming Call: Job Stealer

"Hello?"

"Hey," Luca answered. "How are you feeling?"

I rubbed my ankle. "I am okay, the brace just makes my foot hot, that's all."

"Hmm, the doctor said you can take it off for short periods throughout the day to get some air."

"Yeah, I think I'll do that soon. How about you? How's work?"

He sighed. "Meetings, evaluations, restructuring. Chris left this position a mess for me."

"I forget that you're related to him sometimes. You two are quite different." I closed my eyes to remember my former boss. "He wasn't a bad boss, just an absent one."

"Yeah, well he won't be absent for the holidays, so I'll square up with him then."

The thought of witnessing Chris and Luca wrestling in their bright Christmas sweaters had me giggling. "By the way, do you want to stop by for lunch? I make great BLT sandwiches. I use pretzel bread and toast it in the panini press. It's so delicious."

"I'd love to," he began.

My enthusiasm dropped, as there was a "but" somewhere in that sentence.

He continued, "but I have tons of work to do here. I'll call you later?"

"Yeah," my voice lowered. "Talk to you later"

We hung up, and my heart instantly resumed its loneliness again. There was, of course, Sara and Oscar, both of whom I've been occasionally texting throughout the day. But both of them left me on "Read", leading me to believe they too were busy.

My phone rang once more, but I didn't bothering looking this time since I was sure it was Luca again.

"Hey, Luca—"

"Luca?" the raspy voice asked on the other end of the line.

I stopped. "Dad?"

"Hey, baby girl."

"Wait, one second." I hit the FaceTime button and waited until he picked up.

He did, but the person on the camera didn't look like my dad, and it wasn't because my screen was cracked in three. It was because instead of his usual Knicks jersey he loved to wear, he was in a white hospital smock. Or maybe it was because my father always maintained a weight of 175 pounds, but the man on the screen looked like he was barely reaching 135. Everything was different—the hair loss, the nasal cannula, the hospital bracelet, everything was different, but his smile.

The entire realization that this was who my father had become triggered my teary eyes.

"Aww, Olivia, don't do that to me now. I'm still your dad." He painfully grinned.

I wiped my eyes with the sleeve of my sweater. "How are you feeling?"

"Couldn't be better." He coughed.

"He's in pain," I heard my mom's voice coming from somewhere in the room.

Dad shrugged. "The doctor just gave me some pain meds. They haven't kicked in yet, but enough about me. Your mom told me you hurt your ankle at work or something."

"Yeah." I flipped the camera around to show him the evidence.

"Hmm." He nodded. "So, this Luca character is the one who is helping you I presume."

Heat rushed into my cheeks. "What? I didn't mention anything about Luca."

"No, but you called me Luca on the phone," he explained. "Hey, isn't he your boss? The one whom they wrongfully gave the director position to."

"Yes." I nodded, but I didn't want my father to see Luca in that light, so I told him a shortened G-rated version of my encounters with Luca, minus anything romantic.

"Well, when you put it like that, it's hard for me to hate the guy," he managed a soft chuckle.

Laughing was a good sign. The pain meds started working, but he was still visibly tired. Not tired enough for him to hang up the phone though. So, I suggested that we watch a movie instead. It was a pastime favorite I used to do with my dad during my college years. We'd set up FaceTime and play the same movie on our tv screen. His nurse switched on the room's television to begin watching one of his favorite films, *Rocky*.

When the credits rolled, I reached over to my phone to see if my Dad enjoyed the movie, but he was fast asleep, head held up by several hospital pillows.

"Mom, are you still there?" I asked.

"Yes." She grabbed the phone from my father's hands. "Sorry your dad can't stay up for more than two hours when he's on so many medications. He's scheduled for surgery on the—" she was interrupted but her own slow and long yawn. "Sorry, sweetie, he is scheduled for surgery on the twenty-ninth of this month."

I studied her closely. She wasn't sick, but dark circles under her eyes were clearly caused by many restless nights. She told me that my brother would arrive tomorrow to help with Dad, and that it would free up some time for her to take care of herself while he was around. It was a small sigh of relief for the moment, but it got me thinking that soon I should take time off to go see them.

The remainder of my afternoon was spent folding laundry at my dining room table. It was the only activity I could do that didn't require me to be on my feet, but enough to keep my mind distracted from thinking about my father's looming sickness. A knock at the door interrupted my dwelling.

"Coming," I called out and limped over to open the door.

I opened the door to see Sara and Oscar standing there with two bags from Reggio's Italian restaurant.

"Dinner time," Sara screeched and hugged. "Oh, I missed you so much. Work was dreadful."

I turned to Oscar to confirm. "Was it that bad?"

He nodded. "It was, but it's always like this come this time of year."

"Well then, let me pay you back for dinner. It's my treat since I couldn't help today."

"No need," Sara insisted. "Luca paid for it."

"Luca?"

"Yes," she confirmed as she set my table with plates. "He's here by the way, he's just parking his car."

I peeked out the door and found him walking in our direction with a box in his hand.

"Hey," he came in but stopped within a reasonable acquaintance distance from me. Sara and Oscar knew about mine and Luca's past encounters, but they didn't know about last night, and as of right now I preferred a little privacy.

"What do you have there?" I pointed to the box.

"Your new phone," he answered with a grin.

"Paid for by the company, right?" I shot him a look. "You shouldn't have to pay out of a pocket for an incident at work."

He stood confused by my statement. "Yes, but my family owns the company, which means I own the company."

"Luca?" I pouted. "You know what I mean."

He laughed, and while Sara and Oscar bickered in my kitchen about what to drink, he took the time to move my curly hair from my face and caress my cheek

"It would've taken too long for our accountant to file a claim to replace your phone. So, I paid that out of pocket, but the company is going to pay for the medical bills."

"Thank you."

He bent down and whispered in my ear. "Though I would've paid that too had they given you any ounce of push back."

"It's time to eat." Sara announced coming out from the kitchen with every bottle of liquid from my fridge, milk included. "We couldn't decide on what to drink so we took everything out."

We sat together at the table, and for the first time since I've lived here, I had an unplanned but proper dinner with friends, and one being a love interest at that. Luca and I sat across from each other knowing that it kept Sara and Oscar from suspecting we were together—but it also prevented us from touching. We did pretty well, having listened to the story of Oscar's latest date with his most recent but longest standing belle, Maria. He couldn't stop smiling the more he talked about her, leading me to wonder when he'd pop the question. Sara, on the other hand, had her sights set on having her first child and talked about what her child would look like with her red-headed husband. Both of my friends were headed toward milestones, and I couldn't be happier for them.

Luca brushed his foot against my leg during dessert. I flashed a smile at him and he winked in return. This was our third time doing this. We were ready for some privacy, but Sara and Oscar had been blissfully singing the national anthem off key and out of sync. As much as I wanted to enjoy the wonders of friendship and community, I also needed them to leave, like now.

"Oh, would you look at the time," I pointed to my new phone. "Luca, don't we have work tomorrow."

Luca caught on, "You bet, tomorrow is Friday, and I've been cracking down on lateness."

"Aww, c'mon." Sara put down my remote she had been using as a pretend microphone. "It's only seven p.m." She frowned.

"That's fine, I have to meet Maria anyway." Oscar put on his coat and hat. He was the easy one; Sara not so much.

Sara bid Oscar farewell but made no effort to put her own jacket on. "So, Olivia, what are your evening plans? Want to watch this new medical drama I found on Netflix?"

"Evening plans!?" I repeated and handed her her jacket. "My evening plans are to catch up on work. Luca and I have plenty to discuss about tomorrow's schedule."

"But—" she tried to resist, but I knew the perfect way to get her going.

"Or you can stick around and help us with the presentations, spreadsheets, and—"

Her face scrunched in disgust. "Oh, eww, get me out of here. I had enough of that today." She threw on her peacoat and wrapped her scarf around her neck. "See you tomorrow!" She waved as she departed down my walkway.

It wasn't until we saw her car fully exited my community gate that we turned to each other. Silence flooded the room—there was eagerness in both our eyes.

Luca stepped forward slowly. I should've met him halfway, but excitement glued me to my spot. My heart fluttered at the mere proximity of his approaching body.

His hands glided down my arm. "You're shaking. Are you cold?

"Just excited, I blushed and wrapped my arms around his narrow waist. "It's been a long day without you." My gaze met his.

"I'm sorry, I'm back now." He bent down to stroke my nose with his.

"That tickles," I snickered.

"I can be softer," he whispered as he slowed his movements.

It was an innocent exchange that was enough to satisfy my Luca fix. I leaned against his firm chest and relaxed. I needed to prepare myself for the next request. "Luca, let me go to work tomorrow."

He didn't answer right away, instead combed my curls slowly with his fingers. He was thinking about it.

"Luca?" I pleaded.

"Hmmm?" The word vibrated from his chest.

I peeked up at him. "Please?"

"Yes," he gave in.

"Really?" I smiled in delight.

"But," he warned with dark eyes, "under no circumstances are you to enter the archive room. Do you understand?"

"Oh, don't worry—"

"Olivia," he said in his manager's voice. "I need your compliance."

He was serious; this was boss Luca I was talking to now. "Yes." I nodded.

We walked over to the sofa and sat down for this much anticipated conversation—the topic about *us*.

"So, I want to be direct with you about my past relationships," he began. "I always started them the wrong way, and they spiraled out of control from there. It was fun at first, but nothing concrete, and with you I don't want to risk it. I want to do things the right way this time, especially with you." He paused. "You seem like a person that doesn't mind—"

"Waiting," I concluded for him. "A girl that doesn't mind waiting, you mean."

"Yes." His attention dropped to his hands as he briefly refused to look at me. "It's selfish to ask, I know. Especially because I didn't always wait myself in the past, but my life is changing right now, and for once I think I'm getting this right. I just wanted to tell you, so you knew where I stood. There might be some things we need to adjust, but it's because I want to get things right this time."

There was so much going on in his head and it showed in his tired but serious expression. He pressed his lips into a thin line as he finally was able to look at me again.

"Luca, this is the only version I know of you. So, if you're looking for my answer, then it's yes. I don't need to go any further unless we both agree on what we're doing."

He sighed a breath of relief and his shoulders relaxed. "Thank you." He scooted to the edge of the couch, now ready to get to the meat of evening. "Now, one week ago we had a heated argument in my office. You made an accusation against me. You said I was giving you privilege. Do you think that's true? That I give you privilege above other employees?"

"I mean, I don't know." I scratched my head. "There were some things said that were spoken out of emotion rather than facts, but you and I both know there are things that might become problems if people knew about us."

He nodded and took it in. "So, I must tell you the truth, that night I couldn't sleep well, because you accused me of unfairness."

"I didn't mean that. I'm sorry."

"Don't be," he rushed to say. "Don't ever be sorry when you're holding me accountable. But if I may, let me explain. Olivia, there will be times where you experience privilege because of my feelings for you; whether we go out, or take vacations, or be our normal selves. Because of my feelings for you, you will be given protection, gifts, and other wonderful tangible and intangible things. It is a form of my affection for you, and you're owed that.

That being said, the workplace is where fairness should be the precedent of every decision, but we live in a world of imperfect people, and in this case imperfect directors. That day, I can assure you that I was not punishing the BSG employees for our relationship."

I touched his face, knowing he was suffering from the guilt that I caused him. "Then I believe you."

"However, there might be a day where I do." He looked at me with sadness. "So, you need to tell me if that ever happens."

I nodded. "Is that it?"

"The last thing is about the deal we made."

"Right, our deal, the one we made almost three months ago. I have things written but now that we are—well I don't know what we are yet, so it's best if we abandon the contract."

"No," he replied strongly.

His answer startled me, not because of his strong tone but because of the response itself.

"But, Luca, you remember, right? The stipulations of that deal—if you lose your position, you won't work at BSG anymore."

"I know."

"And how do you know that I won't skew the results to my preferred result?"

"That was the same concern you had when we first made the deal, and when you asked me about it, I said it's because I trust you to be fair, but now I not only trust you to be fair. I am asking you to be fair despite our growing relationship. Olivia, I *need* you to be fair," he begged.

"Luca, what is this about?" I shook my head, confused.

"I will tell you, just not right now. Just promise me you'll hold me to the highest standard, higher than the standard you set for yourself." He held out his hand. "If you still believe that you deserve my position, then you need to show Deirdra that."

"It doesn't bother me anymore."

"It does." He stood firmly on his point. "I can see it in your eyes when you look at her, hear it in your voice when you speak. If things aren't settled soon, it will affect our relationship. Just think about it."

14

G etting ready for work was harder today than yesterday, maybe because Sara was texting me nonstop as I was leaving my house. Nevertheless, I appreciated that she offered to take me to work. Originally, Luca asked if he could do it, but I requested that he'd be my afternoon Uber. It was also an excuse to see him later.

Beep beep! Sara's car sounded like a broken horn.

"Coming!" I yelled. If I didn't get out of my house soon, my neighbors would call the cops on a rowdy disturbance—Sara.

I held my raincoat over my head and limped over to Sara's SUV. She reached over the car's console and opened the door.

"Thanks," I said, getting in and combing away my damp curls.

"Uh huh." She put the car in drive and refused to look in my direction.

She was mad about something. I tried to think of what it was before asking. I haven't missed a phone call or text message from her. We haven't cut back on our quality time together either. What could it be?

"What's going on with you and Luca?" She blurted angrily. "He has been possessive with you lately."

"Umm?"

"I mean I know you're both managers and have that important project together, and I know you two had all that chemistry, but I thought both of you were past that already. I just feel like —" her voice trembled, "you're replacing me with him."

"Sara, that's not it." I turned to her. She kept her focus on the road, but tears ran down her cheeks.

It was time to completely be honest with her.

"I *really* like him, Sara," I admitted.

She swung her head in my direction as she was driving. "You like—"

"Yes, I like Luca, and it's not like these lustful moments. I actually really like Luca, and the feelings are mutual."

"Aww," she cried. She put the car in park at a traffic light and reached over to hug me.

Strands of blonde hair got into my mouth. "Ahh!" I pinched them out. "Sara, we have to go, the light turned green already. "

The line of cars behind us beeped at us to drive.

"Sorry, sorry!" She returned to her wheel. "I don't know why I'm so emotional lately. I'm just so happy for you." She wiped her tears. "It makes so much sense now."

She dropped me off in front of the building. "I'll meet you inside." The moment I got out, several heads turned.

Luca met me at the entryway. "Good morning," he greeted me with a smile but then focused on my foot.

"I'm okay," I mouthed to him. I didn't need to attract any more attention than I already had within the ten seconds that I'd arrived.

He opened his mouth to refute but was called over by another employee. Still, he refused to move.

"You know you have to go," I exclaimed. "You're a very important person in the company."

Knowing I was right, he huffed and walked past me, making sure to gently push into my body just enough to catch me by waist.

He pulled me back up and our chests briefly met, his back hand securing the small of my back. "My apologies. Ms. Kaddel."

He left me both red and excited in just a quick moment.

Sara came up from behind and walked me to an empty elevator. The door closed and she screeched.

"Ouch," I covered my ears. "We're in an enclosed area."

She leaned against the elevator walls, closed her eyes, and slid down to the floor "I see it now—you and Luca."

I laughed and helped off the floor. "You're ridiculous."

She dusted her pants off and shot me a look. "You know what you have to watch out for from now on—Brenda and the snakes. They already hate that you get to spend so much time with Mr. Dreamy. I know you're a tough cookie, but don't let them get to you, okay?" She gave me a hug and got off on her floor.

One day off meant I was one day backed up on emails, approvals, and follow-ups. The second I arrived at my cubicle, Oscar pulled up a second chair for me to rest my foot on and I went to work. I marked things off on my calendar as I filled up my schedule for the next week. I was especially excited to train Team Delta later. Today was all about my department, which has been neglected these past few weeks due to the other responsibilities.

A subtle knock behind me caught my attention. I spun around to see Deirdra standing idly at the entry of my cubicle.

"Oh! Hey, Deirdra," I greeted, but I was a tad confused. Not only has Deirdra never visited my working space. She never meets with someone without requesting a meeting prior.

"Hello, Olivia," she said and let herself in. Her eyes drifted around to my pictures, my computer, my office decor, then back to me.

"Can I help you with something?" I offered.

"Oh, yes." She snapped out of it. "I just wanted to—" She stopped and searched behind her. "Just wanted to—" She searched some more until she couldn't help it. "Oh goodness, Olivia! How can you operate as a manager without supplying adequate seating for guests and employees? Oscar, dear?" she called over the wall. "Please fetch an extra chair so that I can rest."

Oscar could not find an extra chair that would fit Deirdra's comfort level, so he offered her his chair, which she accepted despite calling it a teenage boy's gaming chair.

She sat down, flipped her 80's styled hair, and crossed her legs. "Anyway, I just wanted to check on you to make sure you're okay. Luca told me what happened in the archive room, and we are immediately taking steps to ensure that it does not happen to anyone ever again."

Most of everything she was saying was expected from any company that didn't want to get sued, so I couldn't tell if she was genuine or not. Regardless, I had to play the part and be grateful.

"Uh, thank you."

"Of course, my nephew was quite upset when the incident happened," she revealed. "He's taken the lead to work with our archive administrator to reconstruct the department and how to safely access information. I can't wait for you to see all the ideas he's come up with."

I offered a forced smile. She had to be kidding. I've been saying we needed a new system for archiving for years. I've even gone so far as presenting a slideshow to Deirdra, to which she responded that it wasn't in this year's budget.

She continued about the countless wonderful things Luca had been doing for the company since he started. At the end of it she asked if I agreed, and what was I supposed to say, 'No, I hated it'? It wasn't that I hated it, but that it was my idea first, and she never acknowledged that.

The entire thing brought back my never-ending frustrations with her and how time after time she overlooked my contributions to the company.

She got up and left without saying goodbye, but it didn't bother me since she was never one to say more than what the conversation required. It was actually good that she left—it hadn't even reached noon, but I was already over her.

Oscar peeked in, ensuring that she was indeed gone.

"Do you want your office chair back?" I asked.

"It's not an office chair," he corrected. "It's a teenage boy's gaming chair." He waited for my chuckle, but when none came, he grew concerned. "Are you okay, boss?"

"Yeah." I shrugged.

"Hmm..." He picked up my water bottle and swirled it around. "Maybe you're just dehydrated and need some more water. And you know, the water fountain down by Luca's office is said to be the best water in the entire building. You should take a walk, you know, go try it." He winked and rolled his chair out.

So, I left for the coveted water fountain. It was interesting— the more I thought about it, Sara had known me longer than Oscar, but Oscar understood me deeper, especially at this time in my life.

I dropped my speed when I approached Luca's office. He was in what seemed to be an enjoyable meeting with our recruiter, John. Head tilted, posture relaxed, jacket off, and smile on full display. His smile stretched even further the moment he caught me peeking in. John reached down into his briefcase, and Luca took advantage of the moment. "Do you need me?" he mouthed.

I shook my head and mouthed back. "Just wanted to say hello."

His eyebrows squeezed together. He was trying to figure me out.

John came up with a folder and caught Luca staring beyond him, which made him turn around too.

"Hey, Olivia," he called out. His voice was loud enough to hear beyond the glass walls. "I found you a new hire, by the way. Email you about it later!"

I gave him a thumbs-up and then left, not wanting to interrupt their meeting any further.

From afar, I spotted a familiar man waiting in line to fill his water bottle.

The closer I got, the more I was sure it was him. "William?" I called out.

William turned around, his attention dropping from my face to my foot. "Hey, Olivia—oh, shoot. What happened to your foot?"

"Well, it had to do with a ladder, the archive room, and a folder."

"So, it was *you* who hurt themselves?"

"It was me," I admitted.

His emotion settled in seconds, he felt bad for mentioning it. "By the way, thanks for sharing the spreadsheet template with me. It has made transferring to our new system so much easier."

"Of course. I'm happy I could help. Your manager, Jason, actually has that spreadsheet saved on his drive, but he's stubborn and only likes to do what he knows."

William's eyes burned with aggravation. "He's like my dad! Only does what he knows and won't give anything else a try even if he knows it's better. Working under him is like living back at home."

I let William vent some more as I found myself relating to him during my first couple of months at BSG.

"Listen," I finally said. "Jason fears that us thirty-somethings are going to waltz in and change everything overnight, then put him out of the job the next day. While I understand that's what many senior employees are facing right now, he should still respect you—this isn't your first rodeo."

William exhaled softly and relaxed. "Thanks, Olivia."

"Yeah, no problem." I turned to leave, but he stopped me.

"No, seriously. Thank you. It's been tough these past few weeks so hearing that from a manager is reassuring. You're truly amazing." William's eyes drifted up. "Oh hey, Luca."

The moment he said Luca's name I felt a large, warm body brushing ever so slightly against my back. Luca moved beside me, gently sliding his large hands against the lower part of my blouse.

"My apologies, Olivia."

"Hey, William." Luca's director's voice came on. "Everything okay?"

"Yeah." William glanced back down at me, but returned his attention to Luca. "I was just getting some water; you guys have the best water fountain in the building. Hands down."

"I've heard." Luca nodded suspiciously. "Is that all?"

"Well, Olivia was giving me advice on a situation I've been facing. She's freaking awesome."

Luca gazed down at me, his eyes absorbed with mine as if we were alone. "Well, I'll have to experience it sometime then."

"Luca?" I said loudly hoping to get his attention.

He snapped out of it, turned back to William. "Anyway, I'll have maintenance place the same water filter on every floor, that way you don't have to travel all the way up here for water."

William waved goodbye and waited for the elevator. Luca didn't leave until he witnessed the elevator door shut with William in it.

I chuckled to myself and walked away slowly, knowing Luca would soon follow behind. Once I heard his footsteps, I picked up my pace passing my desk, and into the poorly lit stairwell, shutting the heavy metal door behind me.

It took a full three seconds before the door was pushed open, and a bewildered Luca joined me in the secluded area.

His parted mouth and arched eyebrows signaled an explanation as to why I chose to retreat to stairwell B and not just talk to him in his office. But then his eyes darkened and a cocky grin crossed his face.

He closed the distance between us until my back was laid flat against the concrete wall. His eyes drifted between my eyes and lips, deciding which one to gaze at, but finally rested on my eyes.

"I thought you didn't like the stairwells," he taunted.

I shrugged, "Yeah, well, a guy at work took care of that for me."

"Hmm," he couldn't help himself, and his attention ventured back down to my lips. "Is he nice?"

"When he wants to be, except when another male employee talks to me."

That stopped him. "Was I really that bad?"

"Ehh, you could have added a touch of humor into it. Throw in a joke or two."

"But I wasn't joking," he admitted. He leaned forward and rested his forearm against the wall above me, supporting his weight while he looked down. He was closing in on me, until an unnerving thought crossed my mind.

"Luca," I said.

He froze. Tension wrinkled his forehead, and his brows were practically touching at this point. I pissed him off.

A puff of wind blew through his nostrils. "Why do you stop me, Olivia?"

"Your aunt came to apologize about the ladder accident. She wanted to know how I was feeling." I knew to mention my foot first—anything to do with my health immediately regulates his emotion.

His eyes softened as he glanced down at my brace.

I went on. "She said that you sent her plans for the new remodel."

"Oh yeah, guess she ruined my good news for you." He studied my face, "but it doesn't look like you're too happy about it. Tell me what I can change."

He was serious; he wanted to know what I could suggest to make his plans for the archive room better, but it wasn't about that. Not at all. It was about my plans, and Deirdra's lack of recognition for me.

Me.

It sounded selfish the more I thought about it. It had nothing to do with me. It has to do with the safety and well-being of all employees when entering the archive room. So, regardless of whether it's mine or Luca's idea, I should be grateful that it's finally getting done.

I peered up to see Luca's pondering face as he still awaited my answer. I shook the feeling off and smiled. "It's nothing, I'm sure it's going to look great."

My hands grasped his pressed oxford shirt, and I pulled down. His mouth crashed into mine, causing my lips to instantly separate.

The kiss was nothing like our first, it was a hungry kiss. Luca slowed his movements, hoping I got the hint and slowed down as well. But I didn't, neither did I want to.

I broke the kiss, just millimeters from his lips, to defend my position. "I want to lead this time," I panted. "Let me lead."

Luca searched my eyes, and saw the eagerness in my pupils "Am I too slow for you?"

"Today, you are." I was done with the talking and pulled down for another round. He did in fact let me lead, though I had no clue what I was doing. My hands travel to his chest, then his back, then to neck, then back to chest. I also couldn't find a steady pacing, and I wound up just biting him.

"We should stop," I suggested after giving up midway, "Well, I should stop."

Luca smiled and wiped the saliva from the corner of my mouth, "Only if you want."

"I'm just hurting you," I referred to his puffy top lip. "Let's just call it what it is, I'm a bad kisser."

"Who told you that?"

"My first kiss, Brandon Helen. It was right outside my fourth period Chemistry class, before a unit exam."

"You pass?"

"I failed."

"He's a dirt bag for telling you a lie, and even worse for saying it before your exam. C'mon, let's head back."

I helped him tuck in his shirt while he fixed my hair. I straightened his tie, he fastened my earring back on.

We walked out, though I preferred he stay a while longer to ensure his redness had faded. He didn't care about his puffy lips, the staff staring, or whatever story that our exit might imply.

The beauty of owning a company, I guess.

The day moved on as such, training with team Delta, lunch with Sara; all I was waiting for now was an end-of-day wrap up with Oscar.

But he was still in his meeting with Deirdra and Luca. So, I waited patiently in my cubicle and hoped at the very least, we'd have time for a five-minute chat.

Heavy footsteps approached. Oscar entered with a folder in hand. "Sorry, Boss."

"How was it?"

"Well, they gave me this," Oscar passed me the folder. It was a recognition award from the Scottfield family to Oscar Raúl Bedonalez for outstanding performance and dedication.

"Pretty neat, huh?"

"Yeah, I didn't even know we gave those out." I passed the folder back to him.

"You, out of the entire staff, never got one?!" He scoffed. "That's hard to believe."

"Well, believe it," I sighed. "So, it was just the recognition letter."

Oscar shook his head. "No, it was a lot of things. I never knew Deirdra could praise someone so much. She told me all the great things I've been doing and how much I've grown since I began working here. Anyway, she told me that I was ready for something higher, something she hopes I will accept when the time comes."

"Wow, that sounds great, Oscar," I congratulated him with a loose hug. "I'm happy for you."

"Thank you!" He placed the award down on my table and took a picture of it with his phone.

"Are you going to send a picture of it to Maria?"

"No, I am sending it to my mom. I know it will make her smile, and if all goes well, I will fly her to the country to stay with me during the summer."

There was something special about seeing a forty-three-year-old man get giddy about showing his parents his achievements, especially Oscar. He was in utter happiness by his award, so why should I disturb that with more work?

"He slipped the award back into the folder and grabbed his

coat. "Sorry, Olivia, about the wrap-up. I am going to show Sara my award and then head off for the day. See ya."

"Yeah," I muttered watching him off. "See ya."

Within minutes, the office quieted down. Everyone had left, so I completed my end-of-day routine, putting away my laptop and turning off my space heater. My mind was on autopilot as I thought about Oscar and his recognition. I mean, I was happy for him, he was excelling and getting recognized. It's what I always wanted for him—to go far.

"Ahem."

Luca's voice startled me, causing me to drop my new phone on the ground.

"Shoot!"

He bent down to get it, but I got to it first.

"It's okay. I got it." I sighed.

Luca came back up to meet me, a smirk crossed his face. "Hey."

"Oh hey," I said back, wiping my phone vigorously of any dirt.

Luca noticed my inattentiveness and titled his head to get a better look at me. "Is something the matter?"

"No." I slipped my phone away. "Let's go."

My car was another situation needing to be tackled. The engine hadn't started in several days and it was already sick with the check engine light.

Luca turned the key into my senior Jeep, and after a few pulls, got the door open. A piece of the plastic handle fell onto the ground. Insignificant yes, but, for some reason, my eyes refuse to move from it. Maybe because it was the first sign that this truly might be it.

My arms wrapped around my body as I watched Luca turn the key several times in the ignition. Again and again, he'd turned, each time trying a new tactic in between. He was the relentless doctor, and my car was the dying patient.

He didn't lose hope, though I was already scrolling through CarMax for a standard SUV. Luca glanced over at my screen and chuckled, "Let me try one more time," he offered.

He waited five minutes before trying one last time. With force he pushed in the key and turned back to me. A low but vibrating rumble resonated from the hood of the car. Luca shot me a smile. "There it is. She's coming back to us."

The rumble grew into somewhat of constant muffle, sort of. He got out of the car and held the door open. "Enjoy her tonight," he suggested, "This will likely be her last."

It was only until Luca said "last" did it really hit me—all the memories, not just with me, but with my mom.

"Could the mechanic really not fix her?" I asked mournfully.

Luca pulled away the strands of loose curls from my eyes, revealing falling tears. With his thumb he wiped them away in one swipe.

He shut the door once I got in and knocked on the window. "I'll follow you."

I waited until I spotted Luca's sleek black Mercedes exiting the garage and effortlessly approaching me. He shot me a thumbs-up, letting me know he was ready.

At once my foot pressed the accelerator, and my car jolted forward. The force was so strong, my body flung against the back of my seat. "Ow," I rubbed my head from the impact. Thankfully, my ankle didn't shake enough to resonate pain.

Luca, on the other hand, was seconds away from jumping out of his car to come get me. "Olivia!" he yelled immediately.

I rolled down my window. "I'm okay," I assured him. "Let me try one more time."

He leaned back in his seat, but his voice was adamantly serious. "One more, and that's it."

Come on, come on. You can do it, and she did. A little slow, but she did. We decided to take the local road since I couldn't accelerate past 45 miles per hour. The entire ride took double the time for me to get home, but I needed the extra minutes. Why? To cry. About what? Everything. About my jeep. About my dad. About work.

It had been bottling up all day, and it was time for it to spill over.

I parked the car in front of my apartment instead of my assigned parking spot. Luca rolled down his window. "Are you not parking in your spot?"

"No, it's easier for the tow truck to pick it up," I said flatly.

When I got inside, Link circled around my legs.

"Not today, Link." I dropped myself on the sofa but then felt bad for ignoring him.

Luca came in, but there was no energy in me to stand back up. I could hear him unzipping his coat and hanging up his scarf. I could hear him as he greeted Link and fed my goldfish. He made his way over to the sink and washed my mountain of dishes.

Afterwards, he knelt next to me and unzipped my boots. Long fingers crept around my foot and massaged my ankle with ointment. More guilt engulfed me, for I hadn't even looked at him once since he walked through my door.

He finished, and I sat up. I was met with tender hands against my cheeks, urging me to close my eyes.

But I didn't want to close my eyes, so instead I observed him and he let me. I took the time to study every inch of his face. His hair, which I always thought was a sharp taper at the ears, was actually layered in parts, giving dimension. Just as I reached over to feel it, something caught my eyes. Tiny brown specks sprinkled freely across his cheeks and the bridge of his nose.

"Are those—," I squinted my eyes to make sure. "Freckles? You have freckles!?"

"Yes," he admitted, "with a mixture of acne scars."

"They're so tiny, I would've never noticed. Can I touch them?" I asked excitedly.

He nodded and leaned back on the sofa, ready for a full-face examination.

I scoped out his face topography, studying every pore and eyelash. My favorite part was his narrow button nose that curled up at the end. A very European nose indeed, one that gave plastic surgeons a template to imitate. Of course, Luca got it for free.

My eyes dropped down to his lips. Plump and just pink enough for a satisfying kiss. A dot of dried blood sat on the dip of his upper lip. It's where I bit him earlier.

If only I could heal it. Carefully I approached, as I didn't want to hurt him again, and gave soft pecks around the injury which soon became longer kisses.

It wasn't until my fifth kiss that I felt a response. He gently moved his lips to mine and held them there until we were both satisfied.

He smiled into the kiss "And what did I do to deserve that?"

"Everything," I moved in for another, but he stopped me.

"First, I want to ask you something." He sat up to get a better look at me. "What happened today? You were off, and I know about the car and your dad, but there's something else."

I shrugged, "Life, I guess."

"Hmm, yes but there is something in particular that's bothering you." He curled his lip and thought."Is it Deirdra?"

I scoffed. The longer I thought about it the more upset it made me. "It's always her," I finally answered with a trembling voice.

"Olivia, then you also know what we have to do to make this right? We have to finish what we started."

"But what will happen to us after everything is said and done?"

"And what will happen if it doesn't happen? You'll resent me because of her. So, if you were to ask me, would I rather have *us* fall apart or to voluntarily resign based on our deal? I'd resign every time." He took my hands and held them equal distance between our faces. "We'll survive this, we don't both have to work at BSG, but you *do* have to prove to my aunt if you really do deserve my position. It's only fair."

Fair. That word. All my life I loved it, wanting to be judged fairly amongst my peers. It was the only way I could win in life —no privilege, no leg up, nothing. Luca, however, was genuinely good at what he did. He was a good director. Still, if I were to be completely fair on who is more qualified to be the director between the two of us, it would be myself. Whether it be job performance, knowledge, or experience, I'd win every time, and I hated that.

I didn't want to lose Luca. I didn't want to be fair. Today fairness betrayed me.

15

___

Sleep was never an issue for me, as my workday was taxing on both my mind and body. By the time I lay in bed, sleep overtook me in a mere seconds. Today was different.

It was 3:11 a.m. and I hadn't found a comfortable position to find peace in. I turned to my side and watched Link doze deeper into his feline slumber.

"Lucky you." I slid my hand against his fur.

All day, I've desired sleep for my mind, to rest from the impending board meeting that started in seven hours. The PowerPoint is finished and all the prep work is done, but it's taking every ounce of me not to go over it again.

Some of the board members flew into town yesterday and visited the different departments. They spent their time sharing their extensive expertise, as they would call it, when in actuality they distracted staff from work productivity and deadlines. Thus, Sara and Oscar informed me the new hashtag on slack was #WhenWillTheyLeave.

The thread was quite entertaining based on the screenshots

they'd send me. It also helped preoccupy me from thinking about something other than the presentation.

My eyes drifted back to my clock as I watched the hours crawl from three a.m. to four a.m. to five am. I couldn't remember seeing six. I shut my eyes by then, but I was violently dragged out of my sleep when the alarm sounded at seven. One hour of solid sleep was never a good way to start the day, especially one that needed all my energy.

The morning routine seemed like the only thing that was normal. I kept the makeup as simple as possible, using only a neutral pallet with rose blush, and matte lipstick. It worked well with my shiny spiral curls, which fell just past my shoulders after a fresh trim. It was a bold move—the style, that is, not the length. Straight hair was the unspoken preferred style of the business world, but today I wanted to be as close to my natural self as possible. So, curls it was.

The finishing touch was my ivory silk blouse and gray fitted slacks. The matching blazer was optional, but I wasn't running for president so there was no need to be over-the-top.

Ding.

My hand reached over to my phone.

Job Stealer: Hey, just left the house now. See you soon.

I put the phone down and quickly finished getting ready. Luca was bringing me to work today. My car was towed last week and since then, Oscar and Sara have been rotating driving me to work, except today, Luca insisted that he'd drive me.

Ding. Ding. Ding.

My phone kept going off. Was he here already? I picked up the phone.

"Incoming Call from Mom"

Right. Since I left for college, my parents had a relentless habit of calling me the morning I had something important to do. Whether a test, or school play, or tennis match, they made sure to wish me the best of luck, and in this case, it was the presentation.

"Meow," Link rubbed against my legs. "Meow."

"Okay, I'll feed you already." I placed the phone down, knowing I'd call them back right after.

Once everything was done for the day, and I was sure that the apartment wasn't going to burn down while I was gone, I put on my coat—the red one that my mom got me for Christmas—and tightened my scarf. The finishing touch were my sleek black heels, a risky move after my ankle brace got removed just last week.

"Olivia?" I heard the sound of a door shutting.

I peeked out from around the corner. "Luca?"

He stood at the entrance with a grin, in what I knew to be an expensive Italian suit. His attention went straight to my shoes.

"Hmm?" he moved closer.

"It's only for a couple of hours." I pecked him on the lips. "Then I'll change into flats."

After a few minutes of driving he turned to me at a red light. "Are you nervous?"

"Yes, especially when I think about it, but there are moments when I know I am ready to show how strong I've become as a manager, as consultant, as an employee, and it took some time to realize this, but it isn't about you and me anymore. Actually, it was never about you and me."

The light turned green, and Luca accelerated. "How so?"

"Well, this presentation is really for me to show her. Show her how strong of a person I am, show her all I know and what I can do. It's been brewing inside me, and when she gave you the director position instead of me, I took it out on you, but it was really meant for her." I paused. "So, how about you? How do you feel?"

Luca stopped at another red light and sighed, a deeper sigh than I expected.

I sat up and said, "Luca, are you okay?"

"Do you remember the night when we made our deal, and you asked me what I got out of it? Do you remember that?

I nodded.

"You weren't wrong in your assumptions about me and my privilege. I've given it a lot of thought, and I can't remember a day when I lacked anything, even before I could ask for it. I get it. It is a blessing for sure, but it became a curse—especially when I was young." He pressed the accelerator and continued. "You don't know if you have something because you earned it or because of your family's connection."

"And that bothers you?"

"It always has," he admitted. "I received this nationally recognized award, got this coveted internship, got accepted to Cambridge—"

"Cambridge is a wonderful achievement," I assured him. "I know what I said months ago, but you shouldn't feel bad about what you've accomplished."

"Through many tutors that my parents spent thousands of dollars on." He pulled into my favorite parking spot under the tree, instead of his designated garage space. "What I'm trying to say is, would I achieve all these great things by myself? Am I really great at what I do, or was I just born into privilege?"

That triggered a silence between us. The weight of his consciousness lay heavy on him in a way that proved only he could release it. Now it made sense to me—everything he was doing, this deal, this presentation was not only for me, but for him as well.

We walked hand-in-hand into the building. I wasn't sure about it at first, but Luca insisted that after today it wouldn't even matter. He might not be working here anymore.

We split at the entryway so that Luca could give his morning greetings to the staff, and I could head upstairs.

"Good morning," Sara hollered the moment she saw me walk down to my cubicle.

"Mornin'." I waved back. "You're here early."

When I walked into my cubicle, I understood why—she and Oscar had decorated my space with a *Good Luck* banner, Frappuccinos, and donuts.

"Thank you." I hung up my jacket and grabbed a frap from the desk.

Sara switched a Frappuccino with a store-brand water bottled from my cabinet. "Actually, no Frappuccino for you this morning. We don't want to get your top stained."

"How are you feeling?" Oscar asked.

"Good, I was a little nervous this morning, but it's passed, and now I'm excited. I don't know what the future holds, but I'm not worried."

Sara placed her hand up requesting I stop. "Oh. My. Gosh. Did you and Luca become official? Slack is going crazy right now."

"Sara!" Oscar scolded. "Try to keep Oliva relaxed...but let me see as well. I want to know too!"

Slack kept the two occupied while I excused myself to the stairwell to take my mother's call. I hadn't realized she'd been trying to reach non-stop since this morning.

"Hi Mom, sorry I missed your call I—"

"Dad isn't waking up," she said in a stale voice.

"What?! What do you mean he's not waking up?"

I grasped the wall to hold myself up, but there was nothing to grab—the wall was flat. So, instead I sat on a frigid concrete stair.

"Dad had a bad night," she went on to say. "It started when

his heart rate decreased, and everything trickled down from there."

"Where is he now? What did the doctor say? What's his heart rate?" There were so many questions that were spewing out. The adult in me should've stopped knowing my mom had just gone through hell, but the daughter in me needed to know that he was okay, that he was *going* to be okay.

"They're preparing him for surgery now, the surgery he was supposed to have later this week, but the doctor said he won't make it until—" Her voice trembled and broke off.

"Don't say it," I sniffled, then wiped a falling tear. "You don't need to say it."

She got ahold of her voice and continued. "I've been calling to let you know, since the chance of success is fifty percent. I'm sorry, I know you have your presentation at work."

"No, don't be sorry, Mom. Don't ever be sorry. I'll leave work. I'll leave right now and head over to the hospital."

"Your father would want you to stay. He knows how important this is for you. We both do. Do you remember how we always call before something big happens in your life? So, even though he is not here to tell you how proud he is of you and how much he loves you, I am here to tell you this. Do your best and make us proud. We love you, before, now and—"

"Forever," I mumbled.

"Your brother is on his way now. It's a long surgery, so just come after you're finished. Okay, honey? Love you."

"Love you too."

By the time I came back to my cubicle Sara had left and Oscar was at a team meeting. My body dropped into the chair, and I signed in, not really knowing what to tackle first, emails, presentation prep, or checking off duties on my calendar. It all felt blah to me, like it was insignificant in the grand scheme of life.

"Hey." Luca knocked. I didn't bother turning around since I knew it was him.

"We should send the final PowerPoint to Phil. He'll make sure it's on the big screen, and all the board members' tablets."

"Yeah."

"We should also make sure he has the audio on in the meeting room."

"Sure."

"Maybe we can—" he stopped and swirled my chair around to him. Then he saw. "Whoa Olivia, were you crying?"

He bent down to hug me. It took all of me to avoid snuggling into his neck, otherwise, he would have brown foundation all over his white collar.

"My father is getting worse." I sniffed. "He's being prepped for surgery now, but chances for success are only fifty percent."

Luca straightened up. "I thought surgery was later this week. We were going to travel there. I was going to meet him."

"Yes," tears rolled down my face faster and faster. "But he won't make it 'til then. I need to go, Luca, I need to see my dad. My mom wants me to stay and make them proud, but my heart is telling me to go."

He blinked, "Let me go with you, the presentation is not more important than this. Not even close."

"No, it's something I need to do alone, but you are more than capable of presenting this by yourself." I rested my hand against his left cheek. "Luca outside all of the privilege, the position, everything, you're gifted at what you do." I had to work hard to have the skills I have now, but that's my story and I am proud of it. You're naturally talented, and that's your story. We have two different stories, and they both hold their own beauty."

Luca tilted his face and gave a soft peck to the palm of my hand. When he arose, he slid me his keys and told me to keep him updated.

The trip in total would be just over two hours without traffic. My hands gripped the leather steering wheel. Luca's Mercedes was much smaller than my Jeep, something I wasn't used to. My toe pushed down the accelerator; even after I adjusted the seat to my height I was still not within a reasonable distance of the pedal.

Before hitting the highway, I pulled over to the gas station and adjusted myself for a comfortable, but anxiety-filled ride. I made sure to hook up my Spotify playlist to the top 80's hits before taking off. Dad always liked the 80's songs, "It had more heart than the 90's," he reasoned, especially to my mom who was a die-hard 90's fan.

The music helped since there was no one to call. Sara and Oscar both had busy schedules, and Luca had just started the meeting. He told me to update him frequently, but I was only going to do that once I was sure he was finished.

I arrived at St. Mary's Medical Hospital in just over two hours. The receptionist tore off a receipt tag and handed it to me. "The surgery waiting room is on the twelfth floor to your right," he directed. "Show Security your tag to be let in."

Security granted me access and I was greeted into a semi-full room. All I needed was to find a—

"Aunt Liv!" a young girl's voice called, I turned to my left where my four-year-old niece ran up to me and jumped into arms.

"Oof!" I caught her. "Oh, Hannah you're getting so tall." She started slipping out of my hands so I put her down. "And big. Four years of age is really treating you well, isn't it?"

"Aunt, Liv, I am five!" She crossed her arms dissatisfied. "And next month will be my sixth birthday. It'll be a mermaid theme."

Guilt punched me in the stomach. Right, Hannah was five already, not four. She'd lost her two front teeth, and her voice had matured. Work had entrapped me so much that I was absent for the last year of her life.

A tall, dark man walked over. "Hey, sis," my brother Adam greeted me. "We missed you a lot this year."

The embarrassment really started to kick in. "Yeah, I need to change that. You cut your dreads?"

He rubbed his hand against his head. "A recent change."

"Do you like it?"

"My head feels lighter—I like that part. But it's much colder as well—I hate that part."

"What made you decide?"

"Dad," he answered. "Do you remember how much he hated my dreads, and said he would wait until the day he died to see me cut them off?"

It wasn't until he said it that we both felt uncertainty.

He brushed it off. "Anyway, I cut them off to show him, so he needs to wake up."

"Where's Alyssa and Ezra?"

He pointed behind him. "Sitting with Mom."

My mom spotted me the moment I started walking and gave me a long hug.

She let go of me. "How was your presentation?"

"Didn't go. Dad is more important."

"Presentation?" Adam peeked over. "What presentation? And who is this Luca guy Mom told me about? Do you need me to fight him for taking your job?"

"No," I pleaded. "It's a long story. Let me say hello to Alyssa first."

Aylssa looked up and smiled. "We missed you."

"Likewise." I sat next to her and peeked over at Ezra, who was fast asleep in his stroller. He was the perfect mixture of Alyssa and Adam, unlike Hannah, who was Adam's identical twin.

"We'll have to get a picture of you and the kids when he gets up," Adam mentioned. "Especially because this is your first time meeting."

"Really?"

"Yep, you were supposed to visit after he came home from the hospital, but that day never came. You're always working," he teased. "What's going on at work, anyway?"

For the next couple of hours we caught up on life, his new position as project manager, Alyssa stepping down as a full-time teacher, and mom's new sewing club. When it was my turn, I didn't hold back. I told them about Deirdra, Sara's wedding, my new car needs, even Luca—successfully leaving out the relationship part as I wasn't clear on our title just yet. All the catching up helped distract us from the looming thoughts of Dad's surgery, which was reaching hour seven by now.

Alyssa passed me a slice of pizza that Adam had bought as our late lunch.

"Honey, are there any drinks?" she asked.

"No." He searched the bag. "I forgot. I'll grab some from the vending machine downstairs."

"Maybe take Hannah. She needs to burn some energy."

"I'll go too," Mom offered. "Anything to take my mind off your dad helps."

Once they left, Alyssa scooted next to me and grabbed my arm the same way Sara would. "So, how long have you liked him?"

"Huh?"

"Luca?"

"I never said—"

"It's obvious." She giggled. "When are you going to tell your family?"

"Uh, I don't know." I sank further into my seat. I took the few minutes we had alone to summarize my love life.

"Eeeek!" She screeched in excitement, waking up Ezra in the process,

"What happened?" Adam rushed in with a handful of Cokes. "I heard that from the hallway."

"Nothing." She blushed.

The door swung open, but it wasn't the visitor door, it was staff. The doctor walked over to us.

We shot up out of our seats as we were ready to hear the outcome of the surgery.

"Kaddel family?" she asked.

"Yes." My mother slowly approached her. "How is he?"

"He's stable, but it all depends on the next couple of hours."

Adam stepped forward, "You mean if he wakes up or not?"

"Adam," I nudged him. It wasn't the time to be blunt, especially when Mom was so fragile.

"We need to know," he said.

The doctor nodded. "The next few hours will dictate if the surgery is successful or not. We'll have him in a room within the hour."

● ● ●

It was a quarter past six, and Dad lay in his hospital bed. My eyes wouldn't leave him—they *couldn't* leave him. He looked even skinnier than the last time I video called him. His hair was brittle and barely visible. His face was sunken and his lips pale. His body was completely still except for his chest, which inflated every few seconds.

Alyssa took Hannah and Ezra back to the hotel. They needed rest, but she was glad they were able to stay at the hospital for as long as they had. Adam sat in the corner, cupped his hands, and stared at Dad. His upper body was stiff as a pencil, every muscle locked in place as he refused to relax. Mom, on the other hand, dozed off on the spare bed. Now that both Adam and I were with Dad, she was comfortable enough to finally rest but asked that we wake her if anything changed.

Voices sounded on the other side of the door. Someone was coming—most likely the nurse that came every thirty minutes to check Dad's vitals.

The door creaked open and in came the nurse. Following behind her was Luca, who met my gaze and smiled.

Quietly, he walked over to me, draped his arm over my shoulder, and greeted me with a tender kiss on the temple.

His warmth immediately reminded me of my mental and physical exhaustion. My eyes closed as I leaned into him, resting my head against his chest. His heart beat against my ear like a muted drum, muffled by a layer of muscle, skin, and clothing.

A heartbeat—a sign of life. Something so beautiful. Yet now, my father was fighting to keep his own heart beating for him.

"Hey," he broke the silence.

"Hey," I said back, but I was still shocked by his unexpected arrival. "How did you get here?"

"Uber." He looked over at my father. "You're just waiting for him to wake up, right?"

I sighed. "Yeah, but no sign of it yet. I need some distraction, how was the presentation?"

"It was good. They loved the vision that we put into it. I made a mistake while speaking and was unclear about a question someone had, I thought—"

"No," I shook my head, "I don't care about any of that stuff anymore. Life is more than just a career or a title." I gazed into his soft hazel eyes, the ones that belonged to the man I loved. "I just want to be with you, live life with you, go wherever you go. Luca, I am in love with you."

His lips trembled in somewhat of disbelief and excitement.

"Are you, because that means—" He fought hard against his will to kiss me passionately. Instead, he drew me in for an embrace.

"Ahem," Adam coughed. He stood up and approached Luca, giving him the stare-down.

Luca let go of me to hold out his hand, but Adam refused to shake it, so he pulled it back and the encounter became stiff.

It took me a moment to realize it since I had dated for a while, but this is the moment where I was supposed to introduce Luca to my family.

I scratched my head nervously. "Adam this is Luca, my umm... boss."

"The one who got your position?"

"Yeah, that one."

"Nice to meet you," Luca spoke up in his attempt to try again. "I'm sorry that it's under these circumstances."

Adam zeroed in on Luca. "Oh this is good. Just a couple of hours ago I hated you, but a moment ago you two looked like you were about to have a full on make-out session." His eyes bounced back between Luca and me. "Looks like my sister forgot parts of the story. I must sit down and hear how this came about."

So, we all sat down in the corner of the room and caught him up to speed with the information I left out earlier.

After everything, Adam leaned back in the chair and observed us both. He was clearly thinking about how he'd respond, something he got from our father.

"Well, knowing my sister, I would've never thought I'd see her with someone so different from her in almost every category. But if Olivia has chosen you then there must be something amazing I'm missing, so I give my blessing. Welcome to the family." He finally stuck out his hand for the awaited handshake of approval.

"Thank you," Luca accepted and gazed down at me with hopeful eyes. "We are very happy."

Adam nodded, but soon realized that there was one more blessing needed. "And I'm sure my father would accept you well."

"And I do," a small and raspy voice murmured.

My heart leaped as Adam and I both immediately stood up. It didn't even take a second for us to know exactly where the voice came from. My frail father lay in his bed with a half-smile and slightly opened eyes.

16

The recovery road for Dad was going to be a long one, so Adam stayed behind for the week to help Mom sort out the paperwork and give her proper time to take care of herself. My weekend shift would begin the following week and last until I found a suitable caregiver after he got discharged.

I scrolled through my most recent pictures from the past few days, where in almost every one Luca had Hannah on his shoulders or Ezra in his arms. The moment they met him, Hannah couldn't stop asking him questions, while Ezra would only sleep after Luca fed him his formula. I asked what his secret was, to which Hannah responded that he was a natural baby whisperer. The small moment lightened my heart as I pictured what my own little family with Luca might look like.

Hannah jumped into my lap, crossed her arms, and grunted. "Why are you smiling so much? What are you thinking about Aunt Liv?!"

I couldn't remember what lie I told her, but it was enough for her to drop it and move on. Until later that evening when Luca asked me in private. For him, I told him the truth.

Which brings me the present day. I slipped my phone into the compartment of my newly purchased Lexus as I spotted Luca walking out of his building.

He picked up his pace and hopped into the passenger seat.

"Good morning, I brought you some coffee— Oh!" He didn't let another second pass without kissing me. After the first kiss, he tilted his head ever so slightly and moved in for another and another until we were both satisfied—for now.

He returned to his seat, and I realized that I had completely slouched against the window for support.

"Good morning to you as well, and thanks for the coffee." He smiled. "Are you ready?"

Ready as in ready to speak to Deirdra, he meant. After telling him that I could envision a future with him, we were both ready to do whatever it took to make it happen, but one thing I still needed to do was speak to Deirdra.

"Yes, I want to start our lives together already," I put the car in drive and sped away.

Slowly, I backed into my parking spot in BSG. There was no need to park this far away from the building especially since it was a Sunday, but after claiming it for so many years it just felt right.

It was the walk into the building that felt most odd. For many reasons, the building, all my effort, my career, felt so insignificant to my future. Did it matter? Yes, at the time, but so does my happiness outside my career, and if I wanted to have a life with Luca, I needed to be completely clear with Deirdra.

Luca and I stopped in front of her office. "I'll wait for you outside." He pecked my head and left.

When I walked in, she was sitting at her desk with her eyes glued to her phone. Her office was a mess, filled with books, folders, and random decor she'd piled up in the corner.

She looked up and yawned. "Oh! Good morning, dear." She sat up and slid a stack of folders off to the side.

"Good morning to you as well." I pulled up a chair that was pushed to the corner and sat down. "And thank you for agreeing to meet me on a weekend day."

"It's no problem at all, I wanted to talk with you as well about your absence during the board meeting," she frowned. "Members were expecting your attendance. You made me out to be a liar, you know."

This was Deirdra's way of saying that I failed her. I didn't like it, never had. Usually, I'd make it up to her by adding more to my workload and taking on some unrelated tasks that had nothing to do with my position, but not anymore.

"I understand that I failed you that day, but my father was very sick, and supporting my family is the top priority of my life."

"Olivia—"

"Let me finish," I continued.

The strength and seriousness in my voice took her by surprise. She nodded and let me continue.

"For the last few years—no, since the day I worked here— you worked me harder than any other employee. I strived for this company to succeed every day, even on weekends. I take on work that's not mine, I fill in for other managers. I do everything that is expected of me and more, so when I didn't get the director's position, I was heartbroken and felt used by you."

There was plenty more to say, but I needed to see how Deirdra was taking it, since I planned to explain my feelings in small doses. Her face was blank and showed little to no expression. That was a good thing. After many years of working under her, I learned that it was her way of processing information, so I went on.

"In fact, when I found out that you hired your nephew Luca as the director, I resented you more.

Her mouth twitched. My words were finally sinking in and began to sting.

"Because deep down I knew." My gaze hardened at her. "And you knew as well, it should've been me."

"Is that why you've been so stiff with me?" she asked.

"Stiff is a nice way to say it, but yes. You don't know this, but at first, I started to take it out on Luca. So, he made a deal with me. After ninety days of working here, if he hadn't shown me he could measure up to my knowledge and experience, he would leave the position."

Deirdra was shaking her head, confused. "Wait, there was a deal? Ethically, there should be no deals being made of such nature without my knowledge."

"Well, it was made, and it was between me and Luca. You may think it's wrong, but both of us had our own reasons for making it. However, as time passed, Luca showed he's an amazing, strong, and knowledgeable leader. He does deserve the position in his own right. He showed up to the board meeting, and from what I heard, did an exceptional job. So, because of that fact alone, I apologize for criticizing your decision to choose him."

"So, you're telling me this because you felt like you wronged me, am I understanding correctly?"

"I'm telling you this is because I am absolutely and undeniably in love with Luca. I once thought he was the man who stole my position, and it hurt. It was unjust. But at the same time, it was the best thing to ever happen to me. Anyway, I don't want to hold anything else against you, not anymore. I found happiness in the most unexpected but sucky situation, but I chose him— Deirdra, are you okay?"

"Uh, yes." She finally blinked and avoided my eyes. "Umm, that's a lot to take in."

"Yeah, it's what I've been holding in for a while."

She took a deep breath, and smiled forcefully, another thing she would do if she needed to reset.

"Well, let's start with the position, shall we?"

I readied myself for the debate but was okay with whatever she was going to throw at me. I've already found my peace, and she wasn't going to take it away.

Cold blue eyes stared me in the face. "Olivia, you don't deserve the director's position. You deserved my position."

I held my breath. "Wait what?

"When I hired you six years ago, I knew you had potential and saw you had the will. So, from early on I've trained you in intensity and expectation that no other employee could handle and you executed it all perfectly. BSG has grown in every category since you've been working here. You're both a team player and a go-getter. In many ways, I've always knew Chris wasn't going to last, so I trained you in hopes that you would interview for the director position, but as time progressed, I knew you could do more than just that."

I bit my lip, still trying to wrap my head around everything she had said. "I mean, I *could* do more than what a director could do, but wouldn't there need to be a board meeting and voting to make me the CEO?"

"Already in the works." She smiled. "Well, minus your absence during last week's board meeting. That was sort of my big reveal."

"Oh, I really messed up then."

"It's fixable." She brushed off. "Plus, one of my great grandfather's core values was 'Family first, business after. In any case, the board is aware of my decision, and we intend for you and Luca to run the company together, guided by the vision you two presented. My only concern was that I wasn't sure if you two would get along, but clearly you two get along really well." She raised her brow and laughed.

We both laughed. This was the first time in six years that we had an honest conversation, and it felt good.

"Wait, if you're not going to be the CEO anymore, what will you do?"

"Well dear, you aren't the only one who's found love this year." She passed me her phone and told me to swipe to her Greece album, which showed Deirdra and her new wine-owner fiancé, Elias. I could tell by her ear-to-ear smile that she was undoubtedly in love, a feeling we both could relate to.

I passed her phone back, and she sighed happily. "It's time, Olivia. BSG has been my only career all my life. Nevertheless, I will continue my obligations as a BSG board member but this time in Greece. I cannot fathom being away from my love any longer."

A small knock on the door reminded me of my own love who had been awaiting.

Luca came up behind me and snaked his arm around my waist. His presence was safe and comforting to me, even in the presence of his aunt.

"Did you know," I asked him immediately, "of your aunt's plans?"

"Plans?" He looked up at her.

"Not yet," she corrected. "But now that I told you, I'm ready to tell him as well."

She then told him about the new changes and the new direction. Luca took it well and was even excited about our new partnership. We both agreed to whatever the upcoming season looked like for us and walked out her office hand-in-hand to the car.

After a whirlwind of emotion and one crazy conversation

with Deirdra, I turned to him. "Are you ready for our new adventure?"

"As long as I'm with you, I am ready for every new adventure."

BONUS CHAPTER AND MORE

Want some more?

Check out https://beccasimonebooks.carrd.co/ for Luca POV bonus chapter.

Also, if you've enjoyed reading this, please leave a review on Amazon. I read every review and they help new readers discover my books.

One last thing, get ready this Spring for book two, a small town romance...

BOOK 2

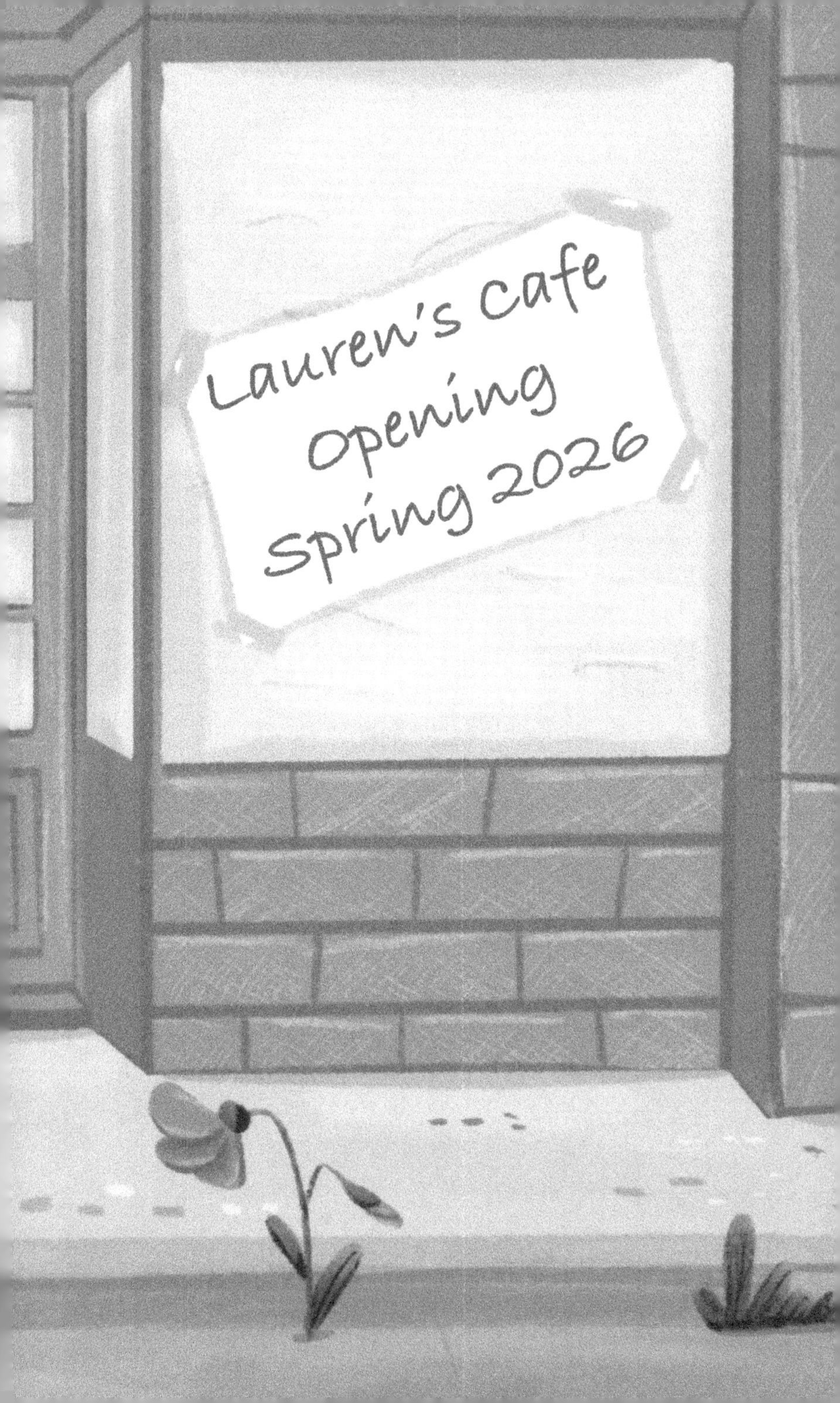
Lauren's Cafe
Opening
Spring 2026

ABOUT BECCA

Becca Simone is an emerging author of adult contemporary romance. When she is not educating children, she enjoys immersing herself in fictional stories and writing relatable characters. Her love of cats and cozy corners gives her the perfect backdrop for creating books that are both fun and charming.

instagram.com/beccasimone93

tiktok.com/@authorbeccasimone